HELL'S KING

HELL'S SON BOOK 3

EVE LANGLAIS

Copyright © 2017, Eve Langlais

Cover Art Razz Dazz Design © 2017

Produced in Canada

Published by Eve Langlais ~ www.EveLanglais.com

E-ISBN: 978-1-77384-001-7

PRINT ISBN: 978-1-77384-002-4

RISE.

Chris—short for Christopher Percy Baphomet—stared at the earth in front of the grave, the freshly turned soil barren of grass. He focused on the disturbed patch of dirt and tried to laser his gaze past it to the coffin a few feet below.

Rise, damn you.

He tried to find the thread that used to connect him to the dead. Looked for the cold tendril he'd taken for granted before. Hoped to see fingers poking through the ground, anything to prove that he'd not wasted his time making a handy-dandy Negan bat—which, for non-*Walking Dead* fans, was a baseball bat wrapped in barbed wire. It lay by his side, waiting to be baptized and given a name. Specially crafted for the next time the graveyard was overrun by zombies. Because it had happened before. Fun times.

The first zombie uprising was how he'd met his wife, Isobel—a hot babe. Together, they'd fought them off. Talk about a unique first date. He'd love to recreate that moment.

Alas, the soil didn't tremble. The thread linking him to the dead didn't give him even the slightest tickle. He'd not been able to make even a croaked cockroach twitch since the wedding.

Holding Isobel's hand—which used to act like some super-magical battery for his powers—wasn't jumpstarting his mojo anymore. Chris had become—*no don't say, don't even think it*—mundane.

Choke.

"Chris!" Isobel yelled for him from the house. Probably because it was Tuesday, which equaled trash day, and guess whose job it was to lug the damned can to the curb?

The Antichrist, the Branch of the Terrible Ones, the King of Fierce Countenance, relegated to menial chores such as the disposal of garbage.

The shame of it.

I'd rather be fighting legions of the undead. Given his dark mood, he didn't reply and instead glared at the dirt once more. *Fucking move.* Do *something*, so he could return to the glory days when he'd valiantly staved off the undead, foiled the horsemen of the apocalypse, and evaded his psychotic mother from another dimension.

As the Antichrist, he used to have such a bright

destiny waiting for him. Then he'd gotten married, and everything in his life became...nice. What a wretched nightmare. He had a home—a clean one with fresh sheets once a week and fluffy towels—home-cooked meals, and Wi-Fi in every room. Guys at the bar envied him his gorgeous wife, who doted on him. A woman who made him happy. A word that should never be used in the same sentence as Destroyer of Nations.

What happened to my destiny? As the son of the Devil, it had been foretold that he would do great things. Reshape the world in a new image.

I gave it up for love.

And at the time, he'd totally been feeling it. He still felt it, actually. He loved his wife, and all he wanted was to have a great new life.

He'd gotten his wish and now had to live with the mindless boredom.

Nothing cool ever happened to him anymore. It probably didn't help that he'd told his dad, Lucifer, to fuck off. And dear old Dad listened. The man he'd never known growing up stopped popping in and made himself scarce.

Chris totally didn't care. He'd lived this long without a dad; he could do without forever.

His sister, Bambi, tried to claim that Dad didn't mean to ignore Chris. Apparently, the Devil was having problems in his Hell kingdom. Who fucking cared? What she didn't grasp was the fact that Chris didn't care that his father had kept a takeover of his kingdom at bay, especially once Chris learned that Lucifer had asked Muriel, his favored daughter, to help instead of his son, Chris.

Then again, who can blame him? What can I do? Without his magic, he was a nobody with only his good looks and charm to rely on. And his charisma was iffy some days.

No one wanted him around except for Isobel. Not even his mother. Ever since the wedding, she'd stopped trying to contact him. The sibilant whispers and deadly encouragements were things of the past.

He kind of missed them. At least it showed she cared.

"Christopher!" Isobel shouted again, and he sighed.

He loved his wife, he truly did, but some days, he missed the excitement of their courtship. The running from danger. The fighting. The awesome sex after battle.

"Chris—"

"I'm coming!" he yelled. "Take your panties off." Because no way was he stupid enough to tell her to keep them on.

He slouched across the graveyard and vaulted over the fence into the backyard of his house. Yes, his house. No more renting shitholes. The one perk of marrying into a rich family—and a bit of blackmail.

What's that? You want us to move out of New Orleans so Isobel can be closer to home? It'll cost you.

Cost Isobel's family a house, and not just any home, a converted church that was still on consecrated ground—which meant no random visits from Daddy. It even still had a steeple, but no bell. Isobel had had it removed the first time he'd gotten wasted and swung from it at 3:00 a.m., trying to wake the dead.

Sadly, it didn't work.

Despite losing that cool perk, Chris was the proud owner of a real home with no landlord to piss him off, which wasn't as awesome as it sounded because it came with a honey-do list. *Honey, clean out the gutter. Honey, can you paint the living room? Honey...*

Was it any wonder he hid in the garage and took a few swigs from his hidden bottle of hooch after he'd slammed the damn garbage can on the curb?

The alcohol burned its way down his throat and warmed his belly. He took another long swallow—his shameful secret. He should add that he didn't hide the drinking because Isobel minded. She really didn't care. The problem arose from blackouts and the fact that he woke up in strange places...sometimes covered in stuff best left in a morgue. Dragging his carcass home smelling of dead dog ass bothered her.

Bothered Chris, too, not that he'd admit it. Apparently, when he blacked out, he knew how to have fun. If only he could recall a single instance of it. Some people would suggest he stop drinking.

He'd tell them to fuck off.

Whether he could recall it or not, he appeared to

be having a good time. And he wasn't about to stop. What he wanted to know was, why did it only happen when he got wasted? Why couldn't he be conscious for it?

Also, when had he become such a whiny bitch?

Because being happy sucked. He took another swig and then hurriedly hid the bottle when the door to the garage began to open, a slow rat-tat-tat as it wheeled up the track, the sliver of daylight at the bottom widening.

Noting a pair of feet and legs, he turned to the workbench and pretended to be working on...nothing. He had nothing. Would she notice?

"Chris. There you are. I've been looking for you. The trash man is coming."

"I took the can to the curb already." Was she blind? He cast her a scowl.

"There's one more." She shook a bag at him, the fact that she could carry said bag to the bottom of the driveway obviously not sinking in. Pretty little rich girl. Which wasn't a dig. He loved that he'd snared himself a princess.

But what about recognizing him as a prince?

Something in his expression must have betrayed his thoughts because her lips flattened. "Don't you give me that look. I've got other stuff to do. I thought we discussed the dividing of the housework."

"No, you discussed. I agreed to everything you said because it meant sex. In other words, you coerced me, and whatever I promised isn't binding." Not being close to his dad didn't mean he ignored the Devil's philosophies.

Dropping the bag, she crossed her arms over her chest. "If you don't want to do your part and help with the chores, then hire someone."

"You know I can't."

"That's right. Because we can't afford to." Because while her family had helped them buy the house, Isobel only got a stipend each month, and a small paycheck from her job for them to live on.

"Not my fault the graveyard business has been slow lately," he defended. Maybe he should go on a murdering spree to drum up business?

"You could get a second job."

The very thought made him wince. Work twice as hard? From birth, he'd been told that, as the Antichrist, he'd have a great destiny. Surely, that came with perks such as a three-day workweek. He'd yet to see any benefits to being the Son of Perdition. And not once had any of those prophecies warned him that he'd actually have to work. As in toil, physically.

The fucking Antichrist lifting a shovel for a living?

I was born to do awesome things. Not dig holes for dead people.

"Dead people make great armies."

Who said that?

Surely, he didn't. Yet the evocative words in his head didn't sound like his mother. His once-chatty egg donor had not said a peep since the wedding. Did this mean she'd given up?

Have you abandoned your poor, baby boy?

Probably for the best. She did, after all, want to use him, which he wasn't keen on. Despite her silence, he kind of doubted that he'd heard the last of her. She'd gone through an awful lot of trouble to talk to him.

Blah. Blah. Blah. Isobel droned on. "Chris, are you even listening to me?"

"Nope." Chris told the truth rather than lie and have his father think he was currying his favor.

Her lips pressed tight. "I said, if you don't want to get another job, then maybe you should talk to your dad, see if he'll lend you some dough."

The only way he'd take a penny from that old goat was if he croaked. "Like fuck."

"Is that going to be your answer to everything?" Isobel arched a brow.

"Are you going to nag me until I agree with you?" He glared right back.

"It's not nagging, it's reasonable persuasion. Why must you be so difficult?"

"I'm not being difficult. The man is a giant, hairy ass." All very true, he'd seen it. "I want nothing to do with him." Eep, teeny-tiny lie. Hopefully, Lucifer didn't notice.

"I don't understand what's wrong with you."

He scrubbed a hand through his hair. "Nothing is wrong. That's the whole fucking problem. Nothing is happening. At all. Life's been boring since we got hitched."

"Well, *excuse* me for not being exciting," she drawled, eyes flashing with anger.

"Don't be like that, duckie. You know that's not what I meant. Just that, since we tied the knot, nothing is happening anymore."

The crossed arms moved only so she could plant her hands on her hips. "Don't you dare blame me for the fact we've currently got peace on Earth."

Did he blame her? He shouldn't. After all, he'd made the choice months ago in that crypt. Love over world domination. Again, at the time, it had seemed like the right thing to do. In retrospect, perhaps he'd been hasty.

"Someone should have told me peace sucked." His lower lip jutted. He sulked very well.

Isobel laughed. "You're an idiot. This quiet spell won't last forever. You're still the Devil's son. Think of this peaceful time as the eye before a storm."

"You think things will get interesting again?"

"I know they will. Have you read the latest divination by Madame Pierrot?" A psychic Isobel's mother engaged to keep tabs on the future.

"Yeah. I read her prediction." Something about the forces of good and evil rising and clashing on the eve of a new darkness emerging. He'd also seen some entrails read recently that claimed that if he became king, another son would usurp him. But that one could have just been paranoia on his part.

"Don't sulk, my dark prince." Her nickname for him. "You're obviously not dying of boredom, given you've come home smelling like a graveyard three times in the last week. Have you been able to get the dead to rise?"

Admit he didn't know how? "Working on it."

"Want me to help?"

Yes. He totally wanted her input. Isobel didn't just have good looks and a banging bod. She possessed an incredible brain. A smart lady who, more often than not, had sound advice. But in this case, her words of wisdom would probably entail sobering up.

Not yet...

"I want to keep trying on my own for a bit," he said in reply to her offer to help.

She couldn't quite hide the hurt that he shut her out. "Nothing wrong with having a partner."

A liberal woman would, of course, say that. Being a bit of a misogynist, he kind of wanted to do it by himself.

"I'm good. And I'll do better about doing my part around here." He snared the bag from the ground and marched it down to the curb. This was man's work. Spit on the ground.

He sauntered back to the garage and noted that she stood just outside, looking yummy in her slim-fitting slacks and a cute blouse. "Anything else for me to do?" he asked. Trimming her hedges came to mind.

"As a matter of fact, I need you to get cleaned up," she advised, eyeing his outfit. "Wear something yuppie from the closet and not anything stuffed in a drawer, would you?"

"Why? What's wrong with what I'm wearing?" He peeked down at his jeans, streaked with grave dirt, a T-shirt Isobel hated—because it was profane, according to her—a red plaid lumber jacket, and steel-toe boots.

"You're filthy. You need a shower."

"Is this your way of getting me naked?" He leered. The sexy kind, not creepy.

"This is not me trying to get laid," she advised, holding her hand up to stem his advance. "We're having company for dinner."

"Not your sister again," he groaned. Isobel's sister, Evangeline, hadn't mellowed toward him at all, and this in spite of the fact that she'd married some dude. On the contrary, she was witchier than ever on account of her pregnancy hormones.

"I invited Eva, but she couldn't come. Something about having to inspect her cat because it's almost tick season. Which reminds me, did you grab that meat from the butcher? He gave me a deal on buying the scraps in bulk again."

"More meat! Exactly how much are we going to spend to feed that beast you call a dog?" A dog more brute than canine.

When Isobel jilted him at the altar during their first attempt at marriage, she'd found Goshen in the swamp. Turned out, he was some kind of legendary hound that had adopted Isobel as his human. It meant wet dog hair, picking up giant, smelly turds, and eyes staring at him when he tried to bang his wife. But it was the growling when she ran errands that made him worry.

"Goshen is family," his duckie stated, not for the first time.

"Goshen wants to eat my face."

"Love me, love my dog."

"I'd love to make him into a coat."

"Don't you dare," she growled.

"I swear, sometimes I think you love the dog more than you love me."

"Don't whine. It's not attractive. Just like that shirt. Really, Chris? I thought we talked about your public appearance."

"There is nothing wrong with my shirt." He peeked down at it, the faded wording still readable—*I'm not a weatherman, but you should expect a few inches tonight.*

Her brow arched. "Nothing wrong? Are you sure about that?" Before he could react, she leaned forward and grabbed the collar.

Rip. The hard yank tore the T-shirt, rendering it a reverse belly top that exposed his upper body.

"That wasn't nice," he declared. "I happen to love

this shirt. Especially since it's true." He waggled his brows.

Her lips twitched. Almost got a smile.

"Spank me later."

"Why not right now? I'm not busy." He was never too busy when it came to fondling his wife.

Before he could grab her, she danced out of reach and wagged a finger. "Actually, you are busy. You need to shower and get dressed."

"Or I could shower and have dinner naked in bed with my wife."

"That might be awkward, seeing as how we've got a guest coming over."

"Since when? I don't recall you mentioning this before."

"Maybe because you weren't listening," said with a huff.

Possible. He tended to tune out things that didn't directly apply to him.

"What happened to your hatred of hosting parties?" Which he approved of given he disliked cleanup. He and his wife, early on in their marriage, discovered they preferred to be entertained in other people's homes.

"This isn't a party, just an invitation to an old friend, but I never thought he'd say yes. He's usually so busy."

He?

"Who?" His gaze narrowed in suspicion. "You

better not have invited my dad." Because he wasn't ready to play nice.

"That old lecher?" She made a face. "Nope. As if I want to dodge his innuendos all night. I reached out to your cousin, and he agreed to come meet you."

"My cousin?" It took Chris a moment to percolate on who that could be. When he figured it out, he shouted, "You invited Jesus fucking Christ to dinner?"

2

"WHAT DO you mean you've made other plans?" His father didn't sound angry. He never did. Or warm. Not even cold. As usual, he was completely neutral about everything.

Charlie sighed. "It's not like you really care if I show up. You barely say a word to me when we have dinner."

"It's not polite to speak with your mouth full."

"It's also not *polite* to ignore your son when he's sitting across from you."

"Perhaps I have nothing to say." Which seemed doubtful. Charlie tried plenty to get his dad to talk. Freak. Do something other than give him that same old placating smile.

"Nothing at all? Really?"

His father paused a moment in thought, stroking

his beard before saying, "Have a pleasant time at your dinner."

"Aren't you even going to ask where I'm going to eat?"

"No."

His father, honest to a fault. Ask him if he thought you had talent as a camel jockey, and he replied, "If all the other camel jockeys were to die, then you'd be an expert."

At times, Charlie wanted to hate him, except he knew it wouldn't do any good. That was just his dad's way.

Still, there was one thing guaranteed to get him going. "Isobel invited me to her place."

"Isobel? Is that the French princess you met a few years ago?"

"No. The Russian one. Her grandfather is Rasputin, the sorcerer."

"I see." Nothing more. Even his father could not completely hide the tiny hint of disapproval, but he didn't criticize. He didn't have to. He kept a mental record instead. Another black mark against Charlie.

"She wants me to meet someone." No need to say whom, there was only one person Isobel would have anyone try and meet.

Father's brows pulled together, thick and bushy and white. "She consorts with the wrong sorts these days."

Charlie totally agreed. "Perhaps she can be convinced to do otherwise."

"She is a married woman. You'd do well to recall that."

"I was speaking of helping as a friend, Father. Nothing more." Only a white lie. Barely a blip, and yet his father would notice—and hold it against his only son.

"You should take a few of the Virtues with you."

Some of Father's more self-righteous guards. No, thanks. "It's a friendly dinner, not an ambush."

"You might want to have them nearby. If not the Virtues, then Michael at the very least. He's good at hiding in plain sight."

Very good. Charlie was always getting into trouble because Michael was a tattletale.

"Such safeguards. I'm surprised, Father. You're acting unusually protective." Most times, Father preferred to let Charlie blithely go off and get injured without a word of warning. His way of ensuring that his son learned his lesson. It didn't exactly endear him. Especially after the crucifixion incident.

"Defending family is an implied commandment."

Father and his rules. The basic tenets of which had evolved millennia ago and still changed depending on the situation. Father had to bend plenty to keep his son from going to the Bad Place. But that courtesy didn't extend to anyone else.

"Your caring just melts my heart." Charlie placed a hand on his chest.

Father harrumphed. "I have to leave. I need to check on the garden."

"Stalking Mother Earth again?" Father had given the Garden of Eden to his old girlfriend ages ago. He claimed it was a loan. One that had lasted eons.

"I would never do such a thing. Gaia is a married woman now."

Married to the Devil. His father's brother. That had to burn—not that Dad ever said a word. Charlie wondered at times if that were why his father had gotten with Mary. Rebound revenge.

"Speaking of women, has there been any word on the entity?" As in the being locked in another dimension. No one seemed to know much about her—or so they claimed—but what they'd seen thus far indicated that the mysterious person, who had control of the four horsemen of the apocalypse, was dangerous. She was also his cousin's mother. His kin being Isobel's husband and Lucifer's son, Christopher Baphomet. The man married to his old flame.

Look at him living a soap opera—which he could say was actually better than reliving an old Bible chapter.

His father shushed him. "You shouldn't speak of her."

"Seriously?" Charlie arched a brow. "No way can she spy on us here." Not with his paranoid father having banned all kinds of surveillance in and around his home.

"You can't be too careful."

"And we can't be stupid, either. We can't exactly ignore the situation."

"As a matter of fact, we can since the situation is still quiet. Despite the seal being broken, my network of angels has neither seen nor heard anything. It's as if she disappeared or went to sleep."

"What of her soldiers?" The horsemen of the apocalypse rode again, or at least they'd been riding. They were silent of late, too.

"I imagine they are plotting to overthrow the world."

"Or not," Charlie replied to be contrary. "Did it ever occur to you that maybe they just want to hang out? Live life?" He knew he did. Screw all the machinations in the tug of war between Heaven and Hell. "Maybe you're all worrying for nothing. Maybe she just wants to enjoy her freedom."

"Enough already!" His father jumped to his feet. "You must stop speaking of her, lest you draw her attention." The closest he'd ever come to hearing his father bark. Finally, something that flustered him.

"You're not superstitious enough to really believe talking about someone summons them." Then again, if there were anyone to be superstitious about, this woman fit the bill. Powerful, with innate magic. From what he'd been able to learn—which wasn't much—

she'd been imprisoned because no one knew how to kill her. Or so his father claimed. Things like her name and why she'd gone on a rampage were still a mystery. Charlie had never met the woman, having taken a break from Earth for a time, visiting with his mom in another dimension. Eventually, he'd gotten bored and returned to the same old thing with his father.

Pacing a bit with agitation, Father slashed a hand through the air—and somewhere on Earth, there was a rumble. "You'd be superstitious, too, if you'd met her. We only barely succeeded in trapping her eons ago."

"There you are, claiming eons again, which makes no sense. She had a kid, and he's only in his twenties."

"Time doesn't move the same for some."

"Or she's not his mom."

Father shook his head, his long beard bucking the trend and dangling past his waist. "She is his mother. She was pregnant with him behind the seal. Somehow, she managed to get him out. And now, it seems she might have escaped, as well."

"So what if she did? If she causes trouble, we'll put her back in."

"With whose help?" Father asked. "The only wizard who had that power has long since left this world. And you know the forces of evil will join her."

Evil as in the Devil and his demonic horde. "Ever think of talking to your brother? Maybe forgiving him, working with him against this threat to mankind?"

Elyon, the name his father liked to be known by—

formerly Yahweh—drew tall and stubborn. A sin his father refused to recognize. He'd based an entire religion on an intractability that wouldn't allow any wiggle room.

"Lucifer has too many sins for forgiveness."

"And yet that hasn't stopped you from playing golf with him." And chess and other games where the Devil cheated to win.

"Golf is a sporting event that allows me to study my brother firsthand."

"Just like this dinner will let me get to know my cousin firsthand."

"I disapprove." Father finally said it.

Which meant he could gleefully say, "Christopher is family."

"The Son of Perdition is destined to do evil."

"Ever think that maybe, just maybe, shutting him out of our life might be the thing that turns him to the dark side?"

"No."

"That's not very Christian of you, Dad. What happened to turn the other cheek?"

"We forgive those that can be redeemed."

"Here we go again," Charlie sighed. He knew better than to keep pushing. On some things, Father wouldn't budge. "Think there's a chance that maybe his mom will show up if I'm there?" Killing her might solve a few problems. Father said that was impossible. Charlie considered it a challenge.

"If she appears, you will leave and warn Michael. He'll know what to do."

"Leave? What if she's killing people?" Charlie knew the answer, but his father's determination to not intervene was legendary.

"If it is their time, then they shall flock to my kingdom."

"And then get jammed at the gate because they didn't pass the entrance exam," Charlie muttered.

"What did you say?"

"I was saying I agreed. Now, if we're done, I've got a dinner to prepare for."

"Try not to get arrested again."

He stalked out of his father's palace in the clouds. *Get betrayed by Judas one time, and Dad never lets me live it down.* Meanwhile, what had his father done lately? His temper tantrum over his old girl-friend marrying his brother had resulted in some pretty big tropical storms. People blamed global warning.

Accuse hot jealousy instead. Except, according to his dad, it was nothing of the sort.

Elyon was peeved without being able to be publicly irked over the fact that he'd waited too long to make a move. And he was also aggravated that his only son wouldn't take an interest in the family business.

Been there. Done that. Father held on to the reins too tightly to share the glory.

Besides, Charlie wanted to make his own mark on

the world. To separate his existence from that of his father's.

Charlie needed to accomplish something epic to make people erect churches in his name. Write books about his life.

Not the time back when he knew nothing, had only twelve disciples, and lived in poverty. He wanted them to write about his life *now*. His success. His philosophies.

An existence that could use a feminine touch. And he knew just the woman he wanted for the job.

Upon arriving at his home, he headed straight for his secret lair. The entire top floor of his house had been converted into a great big man cave. A wide bank of windows overlooked the ocean. Arcade video games, vintage ones like *Pac-Man* and the original *Gauntlet*, sprinkled the outer edges of the space. A pool table covered in blue fabric with chrome edges and legs took pride of place in the middle, while a large, leather sectional faced a wall covered by gigantic television screens. A tablet linked to a state-of-the-art network let him choose any channel he wanted in the world. Gave him access to episodes not even aired, including coveted HBO seasons.

But tonight, he wanted a different view. One he'd scrambled to get installed when he got the call from Isobel.

He only had a kitchen cam thus far, the hidden gadget his employee had stuck in the window the only one they'd managed to install in such a short time. After tonight, he would add more.

He didn't consider it spying, more like keeping an eye on an old friend.

However, the channel showed nothing but an empty room. Not even a peek of the lovely—and forbidden—granddaughter of the grand sorcerer, Rasputin. Father had never approved of their friendship, and it was one of the only times he deigned to rebuke Charlie. Actually, the first and only time he'd *ever* forbidden his only son something he wanted—which was the only reason Charlie had listened. But he never forgot the lovely Isobel.

And now she was back in his life. Calling him!

Surely, that meant something.

Since she wasn't live on camera, he rewound the footage a few hours and sat staring at Isobel as she puttered around the kitchen, making dinner. Preparing for him.

"I'm coming, Isobel." Coming in more ways than one. Good thing leather wiped easily.

3

"Jesus fucking Christ is coming to dinner." Chris couldn't stop repeating it and chortling.

Not exactly the reaction Isobel had expected when she announced their dinner guest. "I don't see what is so funny about it."

"Can't see..." He gaped at her. "You have got to be shitting me."

"I shit you not," she declared solemnly. "Your cousin is coming to dinner." Which was kind of a big deal given that Elyon wouldn't like it. To those who might gasp, thinking her disrespectful, she should note that she was a Rasputin. They knew gods existed; they just didn't worship them.

"Fuck me, Jesus is coming to hang. That's kind of cool." He rubbed his chin. "Can't you just see it? Me and Jesus, sitting down for a beer, chowing down on some pot roast." He shot her a serious look. "You are making your pot roast, right?"

"Yes." Because she knew how much he loved roasted potatoes and gravy. It was the one meal guaranteed to butter him up. Also, the only food she could make with any degree of competence. "As I told you, this isn't a joke. He's really coming."

"Why?"

"Why what?"

"Why is he coming over, of course."

"Because he wants to meet you."

Chris frowned. "I thought you said you invited him, which means he didn't ask to see me."

"Does the how really matter? He said 'yes' right away."

Chris rubbed his chin. "How does one call up Jesus and invite him to dinner? Do you ring a bell and get an angel to fly him a message?"

Her lips twitched. "No bells. Or angels. He's in the contacts list of my cell phone."

Chris rolled his eyes upward, staring at the ceiling. "They have phones in Heaven?"

"He lives on Earth."

"Really?" Chris didn't hide his surprise. "Where? In a monastery, on his knees all day, reciting religious, ass-kissing prayers to his dad?"

For a moment, she almost chided him. However, she had to remind herself that Chris knew nothing of the heavenly side of his family. Lucifer certainly hadn't told him.

"Actually, your cousin has a beach house in Los Angeles. Ten bedrooms, and a view to die for."

"Must be nice to have a rich daddy," he grumbled.

"His father had nothing to do with it. Charlie has been successful."

"Who the fuck is Charlie?"

"Your cousin. Jesus prefers to have people call him Charlie."

"Charlie?" Repeated with a hint of incredulity.

"His full name is actually Charlie Sylvester Shepherd. The first two in honor of his favorite action heroes, and the last because it's like one of his fifty names."

"Why didn't he stick with Jesus?"

"Is that seriously even a question?" Isobel rolled her eyes as she led the way into the house. "You did hear what happened to him the last time he was living in the open, right? They wrote a few books about it. Does being nailed to a cross ring a bell?"

"He didn't die, and he obviously healed."

"Doesn't mean he enjoyed it and wants to risk doing it again."

Chris coughed into his hand. "Pussy."

"Christopher!"

"What? Just saying it like it is. Why hide in the shadows? Be proud of who you are."

"Even if it's dangerous?"

"Especially if it's dangerous. I am dying to do more stuff with my name, but the moment I say, 'hey I'm the Antichrist, son of the Devil,' people freak out. Then the crosses get flashed, and some people start flinging water at me. Which fucks with the gel in my hair." He flicked at the crown of his head, and she snickered.

"You don't wear gel."

"If I did, it totally would."

"Since when do people flash crosses at you?"

"The other day, an old lady in the grocery store did."

"Were you drooling over the fresh meat at the deli again?"

"It was one time, dammit! Even you have to admit that porterhouse was beautiful."

And delicious. "I still think if you want followers, you should start a boy band," she declared, just because she knew it drove him nuts.

"Do I look like the boy band type to you?" With his lanky build and dark hair, he kind of did.

"Just think of the groupie legion you could form, though."

"Of teenage girls."

"If you can get them some Valkyrie training, they'd be hormonal, Berzerker killing machines."

"There is something inherently deviant about that plan."

"Because it's brilliant and a woman suggested it." Isobel couldn't help a smug lilt to her voice.

"Some days, I wonder about you, Isobel. Whose side are you on?"

"Yours. And only yours." What a stupid question.

"What if my side did something you didn't like?"

Sometimes, Chris seemed to forget whom she was related to. The mighty wizard Rasputin, her grandfather, had done some evil things in his lifetime. Truly wicked things. As had her sister Evangeline and mother, Marya. Despite not having done anything truly heinous herself, Isobel was a Rasputin, which meant she could handle blood and bodies.

She clasped Chris's hand and stared earnestly at him. "Don't forget, the side that wins will write the histories and justify the means to the end."

He blinked, those long, luscious lashes sinful on his face. "For a second there, it sounded like you giving me permission to conquer the world."

"If you want to rule it, then I will stand by your side."

"With a knife to go in my back?"

She shook her head, not taking offense at what was a legitimate question.

Chris, for all his brashness, for all his talk of being the Antichrist, was also a man, one who worried about betrayal.

"I would never harm you. We are in this together." She stood on tiptoe and placed her lips on his. A jolt of electricity went through them both. How long since she'd felt it? *Since the wedding...* Odd how it had reappeared now out of the blue.

"You'd let me destroy a nation?" he murmured against her lips.

"If you want to." She wouldn't stand in the way of his destiny. "But you'll need allies. And you won't find them working in the graveyard or hanging around the house. You need to get out, meet some people."

"Apparently, I don't need to leave the house because you managed to get a person of import to see me. Jesus himself."

"Charlie," Isobel corrected.

"Dumbest name ever. Dumbest idea ever. Do you know what Jesus could rake in using his real name? I mean, the merchandising opportunities alone." He expounded on the benefits, his face animated, his hands moving as he talked, his thought process not always aligned with hers, but she could follow it. Even better, he didn't balk at her mindset.

Raised by an evil sorcerer who'd fled Russia after numerous assassination attempts, she'd experienced an interesting upbringing. Some kids dissected frogs in school. She decapitated live ones to brew spells with her mother in the kitchen.

"He doesn't need to exploit his name because Charlie doesn't need money. He's rich. And like I already said, it's not because of his daddy," she tossed over her shoulder.

"When you say rich, are we talking the real kind?

Or that New Age bullshit where you say his wealth is in the quality of his friends and the connections he's made doing good deeds?"

Her nose wrinkled. "Good deeds don't pay. So, no. I mean real money. He's a businessman on Earth, the head of a huge corporation."

Chris snapped his fingers. "Let me guess, he's one of those preachers we see on television. Which I have to say is brilliant. Millions of followers that he can call upon to form an instant army."

She could see the gears in Chris's head spinning, and she jammed them before they could really get going. "You are not going on television as the Antichrist to form a legion of darkness to take over the world."

"Way to ruin my fun."

"Your fun might plunge us into chaos before we're ready."

"Chaos is another word for excitement."

"Exciting is knowing we've got the supplies to survive any siege we mount." Having studied zombie apocalypse films, she knew they needed solar power, guns, and non-perishable food if they wanted to ensure that the end of the world didn't kill them. Thus far, they had...nothing.

"Did you say 'we?'" He arched a brow.

She gave him a peck on the lips. "Yes, we. We're a team."

"A team of two. I might need more than that to rule the world."

True. Hence why she wasn't worried about him annihilating humanity no matter what prophecy said. Free will still counted.

Chris could choose not to destroy the world. But, even if he did annihilate it, she'd still love him. The man might drive her bonkers at times, but despite that, he remained the most exciting thing that had ever happened to her.

And the sex was out of this world.

Mmm. Sex.

She ran her finger down his cheek and almost gave in to temptation. Quick, time to switch gears and veer her mind in another direction. Who wasn't sexy? "Charlie."

"What about him?" Chris asked, his hands on her hips, keeping her close.

"To correct your previous misassumption, Charlie is not a preacher. As a matter of fact, he doesn't go to church at all. He's a billionaire arms dealer," she said as she shoved open the door, entering the house.

The door slammed shut, and she didn't hear Chris behind her. Whirling, she saw him through the window, standing frozen on the other side of the portal.

She turned the knob and yanked it open, holding it lest the spring pull it shut again. "Earth to Christopher. Come in, Christopher."

Chris thawed enough to murmur. "Jesus sells guns."

"Guns and other weapons."

"But isn't that a sin? He's enabling murder."

"It's not murder if he's helping the infidels annihilate each other."

"That's fucking brilliant," he exclaimed. "And annoying."

"Why annoying?"

"Because I can't fucking believe Jesus—"

"Charlie."

"—is more awesome than me."

"What are you talking about? You are plenty awesome."

"For a gravedigger," he grumbled, holding up his callused hands.

"I would have said hard worker."

"Living job to job with no money in the bank and nothing to my name. At my current rate, I'll never be able to give you what you deserve."

"I don't need wealth to be happy."

He eyed her.

"I don't," she stressed. "I have you, which is all I really want. Although, I wouldn't argue with the ability to buy more shoes."

"I'm working on bringing more dough into the equation."

"I know you are."

"Don't placate me."

"Stop being so sensitive," she retorted. "I didn't marry you for money or power. I married you for love."

"Love doesn't pay the bills."

"Neither does complaining."

"Did you just call me a whiny-ass bitch?"

Her lips quirked. "Are you trying to pick a fight to avoid dinner?"

"Yes. It would help if you cooperated."

He looked so adorably disgruntled that she couldn't help but grab his cheeks and kiss him. "I am not canceling dinner."

"Just because I'm agreeing to meet my stupid cousin, doesn't mean I am groveling to my dad for a reunion."

"I would never ask you to do that. If anything, that demon owes you an apology."

"I want nothing from him."

"Well, maybe I do," Isobel sassed. "After all, it was his fault we didn't get married the first time."

Their respective families had forced them into a blind wedding, letting her think that Chris didn't care for her at all. She'd jilted him at the altar and then gave him a second chance if he could prove his love.

He'd turned out to be her hero, they'd wed, and now lived their happily—boring—ever after.

Okay, so she kind of understood why he drank in the garage. What she didn't forgive were the nights he went out to play and came home reeking of zombies and violence.

Would it kill him to invite her, too?

Much like her husband, Isobel felt the pinch of domestic bliss. She just didn't bitch and moan about it all the time. A Rasputin never revealed their emotions. Unless it involved scorn and anger. Evangeline, her sister, excelled at that.

"Hell will freeze over before I ask Lucifer for shit," Chris grumbled.

"Um, you do realize it's happened before. It could happen again."

"Don't remind me. I swear, if I hear one more time how Muriel saved fucking Hell, I'm gonna go postal."

"It's not her fault she's the one your dad calls."

"I'll blame her if I damn well want to."

"Fine, blame your half-sister for things she doesn't control. What I'd like to know is why you're ignoring Bambi, too. She called again."

"Did you tell her I was busy?"

"I told her you were whacking off in the garage because you're an oversexed perv like your dad."

He blinked. He always did when she threw out ribald statements with a straight expression. Inside? She died of laughter.

"You're not funny," he grumbled, a hint of a smile on his lips.

"How long are you going to keep avoiding your family?"

"As long as I damned well please."

"What about Lucinda's birthday?" Muriel's daughter, and his niece—cute as a button with her dimpled smile. She was also a holy terror with too much innate power that some likened to an atomic bomb in a pink bow.

"What about the birthday?"

"We were invited."

"I'm busy."

"I haven't told you the date yet."

"Doesn't matter," Chris muttered.

His reaction to his siblings fascinated Isobel because she could see his longing for family; yet at the same time, he couldn't help the jealousy. He struggled, especially with Muriel, who had been raised by Lucifer and was the one his dad called when trouble arose. The perfect child, as Chris sneered. The sister he wanted to love but hated too much.

As for Bambi, she'd not had it easy growing up. Perhaps that was why Chris related better to her. But ever since the wedding, he'd avoided his elder sibling. Isobel had yet to figure out why but planned to meddle if for no other reason than for something to dull the boredom of her HEA.

"When is Hay-zus coming?" he asked, stripping his shirt and pitching it in the direction of the laundry room across the kitchen.

"He is not tanned enough to pull off that version of his name," she commented, stooping and grabbing his shirt to toss it right into the washer. "And I told him about six."

"It's five now. Plenty of time." He waggled his brows and looked way sexier than that move warranted.

"It is not enough time. I've got to get dinner ready."

He peeked at the stove. "Roast and potatoes are in the oven. You need thirty minutes for Yorkshires. That gives us half an hour. Which is about twenty-five minutes more than we need."

Some might think her deprived because he'd only promised a five-minute wonder, but they'd obviously never slept with Chris. Better not either, or she'd kill them.

She didn't need a ton of foreplay to get where she needed to be. Even the thought of sex with her husband wet her panties.

Her fresh panties. "I'm already showered and dressed." She skimmed her hands down her flowered blouse tucked into slacks.

His arm curled around her waist and dragged her close, his bare chest a heated tease. "Is that a challenge? I'll gladly take them off you."

And not care what happened to her clothes in the process? "Don't you dare. These are my favorite pants." It had taken her an hour to iron them and get the perfect crease down the front of each leg.

"Then strip, wife. Strip for me."

The rumbled demand brought a deep shudder, along with hot desire.

She shoved away from him and caught his gaze,

stared at his dark eyes flecked with red. The planes of his face sharp, the new, short beard and mustache a hot addition. It brought him going down on her to a whole new level.

A flick of her fingers released a button from its loop. Then another. The fire in his gaze intensified and licked outward. Her lips parted as she bathed in the heat.

Her blouse fluttered to the floor, followed by her pants. He reached for her. She danced out of his way and bolted for the stairs to the second floor with him hot on her heels.

He caught her just inside the bathroom. Crushed her to him and kissed her, the hard press of his lips pure, decadent pleasure.

She wrapped herself around him, arms clamped behind his neck, legs wrapped around his shanks.

The rip of her panties brought a quiver. A gasp escaped her at the coldness of the granite counter under her ass.

A hand wrapped in her hair, dragging her back, exposing her to his gaze. To his touch...

The hot latch of his mouth on a breast, the cup of her brassiere shoved to the side had her moaning his name.

"Chris."

He bit down on her nipple.

"Oh, fuck," she gasped.

But this was just the start. He played with her

breasts, a master when it came to arousing her. His mouth sucking wetly, his bites just hard enough to tease, the way he made her feel pure excitement.

"Now." Her pussy clenched and quivered. It needed something inside. Something hard.

His fingers brushed against her as he inserted his hand between their bodies to undo his pants. He didn't strip them, merely shoved at them enough to expose himself.

The swollen tip of him rubbed against her. Right against her clit.

"Chris!" She put an edge on the word, needing him.

He gave it to her, slamming his shaft home, drawing a sharp cry. The sudden widening also triggered her pleasure. She tightened, and he withdrew and then wedged his way back in. She clawed at his shoulders as he pushed in again then pulled out. Toying with her orgasm. Extending it so that she couldn't even get a sound past her tongue.

She totally blanked out, a disembodied spirit of contentment that was joined by another, the pair of them twining, perfectly matched.

Soul mates.

They came back to their bodies and reality. She leaned forward and kissed his chest. "Epic, babe. Really was, but I have to get ready. I'll shower first." She made to push away, but he pulled her close. Held her in a hug.

"I love you, Isobel. No matter what stupid thing I do, remember that."

"Uh-oh. Is this your way of warning me you're planning something stupid?"

"Have you met me? I don't plan it; it usually just happens."

That used to be true. But they'd had months of normalcy. Time to get over the action and adventure they'd gone through, much of it life-threatening.

She missed the adrenaline. Which was probably why she'd called Charlie and told him to come over.

Dinner could prove interesting. And if by some chance it wasn't, then she could always tell Chris about the time at summer camp when she'd dated Charlie and used to sneak out of her cabin at night to meet him.

Am I insane? Why would I tell him that? Chris possessed a pretty big jealous streak. Telling him would...liven things up. And, surely, he wouldn't kill family?

4

KILL ME NOW.

Chris delayed as long as he could. Not out of cowardice but because he'd finally gotten past level thirteen hundred and something in Candy Crush. Damn those conveyor belts and chocolate pieces.

The peal of the doorbell startled him just as a bomb on his tiny screen exploded. It was followed by some woofing as Goshen pretended to be an actual dog.

No more hiding upstairs. He'd have to make an appearance.

Have to. What a joke. He didn't *have* to do anything.

But Chris had waited too long to slip away unnoticed. If he went downstairs now, he'd have to meet his dumbass cousin. He should climb out a window and hang in the city for a few hours instead. Let Isobel entertain Jesus, who would surely bore her to tears. With Jesus as the son of his goody-two-shoes uncle— God, Elyon, whatever the fuck he called himself, who couldn't be bothered to meet a nephew before declaring him evil—Chris would wager he'd be sleeping of boredom before dessert.

Leaving would spare him that torture, and if his wife didn't like it, then she could kiss his ass. Not yet a hairy posterior, but he feared the future. He'd seen Lucifer's butt, the strands dark and wiry, making the prospect frightening.

If ever there were a time to conjure a portal, it was now. He stretched out his hand and called to the Force.

Nothing.

He drew circles in the air. Danced in place. Glowered. Didn't even manage the slightest ripple.

Disappointing but not unexpected. His magic betrayed him. But there was still a window. He contemplated his escape when he heard something.

A giggle.

The sound hadn't come from him, and they'd gotten rid of all the ghosts when they moved in. He frowned as the sound occurred again. Was that his wife tittering downstairs? Their guest had arrived. Probably just being polite.

When she laughed again, he made his decision.

I'll meet this damned cousin, but after, Isobel and I will be having a talk. It was up to Chris, not her, when and where and *if* he met his family.

Despite her instructions to dress nicely, he eschewed boots or socks, wore his comfiest pair of jeans with holes all over them and a grease stain on the thigh, and a tight T-shirt that delineated his chest. He might not have money, but he at least had a pumped body. Modesty was something for those less great than he.

Chris took the stairs down, debating anew whether he should escape when he heard a voice. A man's voice. Deep and smooth like those radio guys at night.

"Isobel, I have to say, you're looking more beautiful than I recall."

A line if Chris had ever heard one.

"Oh, Charlie. You're such a flirt," purred his wife.

What the fuck? She usually only uses that voice on me. He frowned and kept going down the stairs, unable to see anything until he turned the corner.

"It's not flirting if it's the truth."

Gag.

"I'm so glad you could come for dinner," Isobel said.

"As if I'd say no. And judging by the delicious smell, I made the right choice."

"Oh, it's just something I threw together." A modest reply in a sexy tone that Chris knew all too well.

He pressed his lips together tightly and paused on the last step. *Is it me, or is my wife flirting with the dude?*

"When I said I smelled something delicious, I didn't mean the roast."

Fucker was definitely flirting. *Not in my house.*

Chris turned the corner and saw a guy about his height—six feet plus—his short, sandy-blond hair standing atop his head in a thick ruff, and day-old scruff on his face. Casual yet calculated disarray. The dude wore a designer shirt that possessed artful grunge marks and gouges done for maximum effect yet still managed to look expensive.

The jeans the fellow wore low on his hips were even more comfortable-looking than his own. And he'd kicked off unlaced, brown suede, construction-style boots.

The fucker wasn't ugly, and he had a physique to rival Chris's. This couldn't be...

Isobel cast him a glance. "Chris, there you are. I'd like you to meet an old friend and your cousin—"

"You are not Jesus." The words just spilled out of Chris. The fellow looked too disreputable. Shouldn't God's son look more...dorky? Ugly? Less handsome so his wife wouldn't notice?

It didn't help his attitude to see Goshen leaning against the guy, giving him puppy eyes instead of the bloodshot, Cujo version he leveled at Chris.

"I am Jesus, in the flesh, brother." The man held out his hand. "Pleasure to finally meet you."

Chris kept his hands tucked by his sides. "I am not your brother."

"Cousin, brother, doesn't matter. We're family."

"I don't need family."

"We all need someone to lean on." Jesus smiled as he grabbed his hand and shook it. Firmly. "You ever need a helping hand, you call me."

Chris didn't believe it for a minute. "I don't think your dad would like that."

"No, he probably wouldn't, just like Uncle Luc would probably have a fit if I helped you move a couch or bailed you out of jail." Jesus shrugged. "I'm kind of over what they might think."

The words could have been his. "What makes you think I'm the one who'd need bail money?"

Jesus smiled. "Because I've never been caught."

The implication almost brought a smile, but then Chris caught himself. This was Jesus fucking Christ. Not some hoodlum on the wrong side of the church. His idea of delinquency was probably drinking the wine before service or ogling a set of tits.

Clap. Isobel caught their attention. "How about we leave your fathers outside for the night? You're both grown men who can decide for yourselves who you associate with."

"She has a point. But I think we should post pics on Hellagram about what good, clean, wholesome fun we're having. Lucifer would hate it," Chris mused aloud.

"My father would hate it more," Jesus added. "He

warned me to stay away from you because you'd likely be a bad influence."

Chris liked to think he was a bad influence, too. "Isn't disobeying your father like breaking one of those commandment things you have?" There were ten of them if Chris recalled correctly.

He made a note to start his own fucking Bible. The *Antichrist's Bible for Common Sense and Minion Worship*. The title might suck, but the knowledge he'd impart would be epic.

"You mean those impossible rules?" Jesus rolled his eyes and managed to look cool doing it, the fucker. "If you obey them all, you'll want to kill yourself. Except, that's a sin so you're screwed."

"A tough religion."

"It's a cult for the masochists, and it's all a joke. Those rules, the ones that first emerged on stone tablets and then became the cornerstones of a few religions... they were my idea."

At that, Chris exclaimed, "Bullshit. Everyone knows God told Moses—or was that Peter? Some dude at any rate—about them."

"My dad was too busy sulking about sin in the world. He'd thought everyone would behave like a good flock of sheep after the Flood, but the same sins returned. He began to lose followers. Evil took over. Since he wouldn't act, I did. The people needed guidance."

Isobel cleared her throat. "Um, history says Moses

was given the commandments, and he existed well before your birth."

"My human birth. I existed before that as part of my father."

Chris couldn't help a whistle. "Holy shit, dude, you remember being a spermatozoon in your father's nut sac? That's gotta be traumatizing."

Isobel snickered and quickly turned.

Jesus went slack-jawed for a moment before grinning widely. "Never thought of it like that. I can't wait to use it on my father."

"Who art in Heaven," Chris sang.

"Chris!" Isobel hissed.

"What?" he asked, looking anything but innocent.

"Are you high?"

He didn't lie. "A little." Since Isobel freaked when he smoked in the house—*it smells like a skunk died in here*—he kept edible pot gummies inside for the times he needed a quick fix. But the mellow buzz wasn't enough for him to process the fact that he was hanging with Jesus fucking Christ. A legend.

"Don't give him heck, Isobel." Jesus patted him on the shoulder. "Nothing wrong with imbibing what nature has given us. I, too, like the liberating relaxation of a good bud."

Chris sat down, hard, blown away by the fact that Jesus was one of the kids behind the school smoking dope. *He's cool like me.* Which seemed suspicious. He narrowed his gaze. "You are too cool to be Jesus." The honesty he kept spilling must be driving his dad nuts in Hell.

"I try to keep things real."

"Real? Or rebellious? Sounds to me like someone has Daddy issues. Selling weapons that are only good for killing. Hanging out with me."

"Screw expectations. Look at you. Living on Earth, in a house, on consecrated ground, with a job instead of sitting on a throne in Hell."

For a moment, he could picture it, seated on a massive throne perched on a dais, an orange glow around him. Atop his head, a metal crown, lopsided for the cool factor.

That could be me. King. King of everything.

Isobel touched his arm. "Chris?"

He shook off the reverie. "Yeah, I don't know about being Hell's King. I hear the Wi-Fi sucks in the Pit. How is it in Heaven?"

"It's like a never-ending perfect, sunny day. Ideal temperature. Blue sky. Clean streets. Fresh air."

"I was asking about the Wi-Fi."

"Oh," Jesus said, appearing startled. "It's great, brother. Five bars everywhere you go."

"Figures."

"You could install more cell towers."

"In Hell?" Chris stared at Jesus, wondering if the guy were fucking with him. Probably. "I am not living down there. Because I am not going to become its king."

"If you say so, brother."

"I think I need a beer." Chris headed for the fridge.

"Make that two," Jesus, of course, said.

"How old are you?" Chris asked, head in the fridge, looking for the brown bottles Isobel had stashed in the back.

"Old enough to drink." Said with a chuckle.

"Seriously, though, how old? Counting sperm years."

Chris turned and flicked the neck of each bottle off the granite countertop, popping the lids and causing Isobel to shriek, "How many times have I told you not to do that?"

"Spank me later," he said with a wink then set the bottles down on the table.

Jesus curled his hand around one and dragged it closer saying, "I've not kept track. Age is irrelevant when you're a god."

"Don't you mean half-god?" Chris replied before taking a swig. "Your mother was human." Whereas both his parents were not.

Jesus shook his head lightly. "Ah, dear Mary. A lovely woman. Sweet mother for the short time she cared for me, but that's about it. I carry very little of her within me."

"Is she in Heaven with you?" Must be nice to have one's mother around.

"She used to be. Mary left after a century or two."

"Left to go where? Hell?" He said it as a joke, only

Jesus wasn't laughing. "Wait, are you telling me she voluntarily chose to go to that cesspit?"

"Not quite Hell, but nothing as perfect as Heaven either. She went to another plane, somewhere primitive and rarely open to man. I am tempted to visit now that the doors of Limbo have opened again. Once more, the way station is a passageway to other worlds."

What the fuck is Jesus talking about? Other planes? Passageways elsewhere? Chris had so many questions and too much male pride to ask them. It would probably end up being his downfall. His tomb would read: *Here is buried a dumbass. He'd rather die of starvation and dehydration than ask for directions.*

He really needed to change that mindset because he was woefully undereducated when it came to the world his father, sisters, and cousin lived in.

How had he ever thought he could conquer the world, let alone Hell? They were much more vast and complex than his foster mother, Clarice, had ever led him to believe.

"Your mom ditched you, too, eh?" Chris drained his beer, set it down, and then hit the fridge for a fresh pair. He cracked the tops by hand this time since Isobel still grumbled and currently held a large knife to test the potatoes. Never a good idea to tempt the woman who beat him soundly at darts every time they played.

"Mary didn't leave me as young as your mother left you," Jesus noted, taking the beer.

"Mine didn't have much of a choice, given they

banished her psychotic ass to an alternate dimension. Pretty sure she's stuck there, which is probably a good thing. She's a little crazy." Chris circled a finger beside his temple in the universal sign.

"Aren't they all, brother?" Jesus inclined the brown bottle, and Chris snickered then outright laughed when Isobel cuffed him.

"Not funny, you two. We are not all crazy."

"Your sister is," Chris reminded.

Jesus sat up and smiled. "Ah, yes, dear Evangeline. She could make a grown man cry."

The mention made Chris frown. Just how well did Jesus know his wife and her family?

Isobel, for her part, bustled around. "Eva is still the wickedest witch around. And if you don't make yourselves useful, I'm going to give her a shout and tell her you were mean to me."

"Don't you fucking dare." The last time Isobel had sicced her sister on him, Chris had gotten stung on the ass. Both cheeks. Couldn't sit comfortably for days.

"Set the table and uncork the wine, and I won't resort to drastic measures."

"See what I mean?" Chris said in a mock whisper to Jesus. "All fucking nuts."

There was much laughter at the remark. Even Isobel snickered as she mock held up the knife. It set the tone for the evening.

The dinner passed better than Chris would have ever expected. He'd come into this soiree wanting to hate Jesus. But the fellow turned out to be pretty damned likeable. His sense of humor sharp. His ability to drink beer matching Chris's own. And he provided some sweet bud to smoke after dessert.

The mellowness had them both sitting in the backyard, splayed on lawn chairs, the erratic line of solar-powered lights dotting only sparse sections of the short, white picket fence. It wasn't a very good or practical fence. Not even waist-high. It wouldn't stop anyone but a small dog, yet it served as a visual marker to the mourners that their yard wasn't part of the graveyard. Although he was pretty sure more than one body was buried in the yard itself, especially under those flourishing rose bushes. At times like these, the booze and herb relaxing him, it almost felt as if he could reach down and snare the threads that would animate their decaying bodies.

Jesus took a swig of beer. "I have to say, you're the first person I've met who lives in a graveyard." Noted in a whispery voice as Jesus held in some smoke before he handed back the joint.

"I like it out here. Property prices are low. The neighbors are quiet." Which sucked, actually. He missed fighting the dead.

"Who says you've stopped?"

The voice in his head made him blink. His vision blurred, and his cousin turned into a pair.

"You're not what I expected." Jesus crossed his arms over his chest as he stared up at the sky.

"I know, better looking than you thought."

A snort escaped Jesus. "You are funny, too. It's a shame we're supposed to be enemies."

"Don't have to be," Chris slurred, taking another swig of his beer. "I, for one, don't intend to do anything my dad wants."

"Mine doesn't pay attention to anything I do. He's a tad self-absorbed."

"Mine meddles."

"At least he pays attention."

Used to pay attention. Since Chris's wedding, they'd not talked much. After his dad had gotten married and declared Gaia pregnant? Not at all.

That lack of communication meant being on the outside looking in. Or, in this case, hearing secondhand about the battle at sea in Hell and his sister's epic arrival to then save the day. In a chariot drawn by fighting dolphins.

By then, she'd also had a harem of four men.

Overachiever.

Chris wasn't the type to try and ass-kiss his way into his father's good graces. He hated the man. Had no interest in a relationship, especially since he needed to kill his father to take over Hell.

Exactly how did one kill the Devil?

And should it matter if the Devil was his father?

The question required more thought.

The joint, tightly rolled with a cardboard filter to avoid a mouthful of bud, was passed back and forth, the acrid yet aromatic smoke filling his lungs, spreading bone-melting euphoria.

It was that mellow feeling that probably had him misunderstanding Jesus's next words.

"What did you say?"

"I said, I'm glad you managed to see past the fact Isobel and I hooked up as teens. Very mature of you, bro." Jesus offered him a fist to bump.

Chris looked at it. Then the handsome guy.

Who used to date his wife.

He didn't remember jumping out of his chair, but he did enjoy the meaty sound of his fist hitting Jesus in the face.

5

"STOP IT," Isobel yelled, which was about all she could do.

The men grappled on the terrace—the word giving it more grandeur than it deserved since it was comprised of two-by-two concrete squares with moss growing in the crevices. Fists flew, bloodying lips, bruising flesh, and all because Chris had a jealous fit.

"Stop that right now!" She stamped her foot, which did nothing. No surprise. So she did what any responsible pet owner would. She grabbed the hose, turned on the cold water, and doused them both.

The men split apart, snarling.

"Enough." She held the nozzle, aimed and ready to spray. "I am not afraid to use this again."

"He started it," Charlie said, pointing his finger.

"Fucking right, I did." Chris flashed a middle finger.

Isobel glared. "Actually, you started this spat, Charlie, by intentionally spilling the beans about the fact we dated as kids." No point in hiding it now. "Leave."

"Yeah, get the fuck off my property before I demolish that pretty face of yours," Chris snapped before stalking into the house.

"Christopher." She tried to plead with him, but he didn't turn around.

"Yeah, Christopher, come back. Don't go off and pout," Charlie exclaimed in a high-pitched voice.

It didn't help, and her husband slammed the back door shut.

Given the reason for her husband's ire stood there smirking, she slugged Charlie in the arm. "Why would you do that?"

"Do what? Tell the truth?"

"You didn't have to antagonize him. You could see he was upset."

"So am I. He's got a hard left hook." Charlie rubbed his jaw.

She showed him no sympathy. "Which you deserved. You should go. I need to talk to Chris."

"You expect me to leave with him so angry?"

Jealous angry. A tiny part of her reveled in the fact that he went a little crazy when it came to her.

"Chris won't hurt me." But she couldn't guarantee Charlie's safety.

"I assumed you'd told your husband about us. Sorry."

Somehow, she doubted that. "My fault. I should have told Chris we used to date, but I knew if I did, he'd never agree to meet you." Or he'd kill Charlie. He was cutely possessive like that.

"Despite the fact he's got Neanderthal jealousy issues, he's an interesting guy. I can see why you married him."

"Yeah, well, I don't know how long that's going to last. Something is going on with him." She worried about her husband. He'd been behaving oddly the last few weeks.

"You said he's been sneaking out." Charlie suddenly got the crux of the real reason she'd invited him to dinner.

"Only when he gets drunk and high." Which seemed to be the catalyst for setting him off.

"That would be when his usual mental defenses are at their lowest."

Isobel didn't like the implication. "He's not being possessed."

"Would you prefer I say mentally guided by someone else?"

Her lips pursed. "I asked Chris, and he said he hasn't heard his mother since the wedding." Which was a good thing. The woman—freaky monster from another dimension—liked possessing the dead.

"So he claims."

"He wouldn't lie to me."

"Lying would be a natural thing for the son of the Devil."

"To anyone else, yes, but Chris doesn't lie to me." If anything, he was honest to a fault.

"Honey, how do these pants look on me?"

"Like your ass is flat, and while you're changing them, you might want to swap that shirt. It gives you linebacker shoulders."

"If your husband isn't lying, then where is he going at night?"

"I don't think he knows." Each time, the morning after when she asked him how his night was, he replied, "Slept like a baby with a brandy soother."

Either he lied, or he truly thought he slept.

Which was why the last time he'd gotten drunk and sleepwalked, she'd tried to follow him, only to get stymied when he took their one and only means of transportation. Their secondhand, piece-of-crap car.

Relaying the dilemma to Evangeline, Isobel had been offered the use of her sister's broom, but given that Isobel's magic was still in a wonky, learning stage, she didn't trust herself on a slim rod suspended dozens of feet in the air.

As for using a regular car with her sister driving— because no way was Eva loaning Isobel her wheels after what had happened to Isobel's last car—she didn't trust Eva to keep Chris alive if she didn't like what they discovered.

Hence why she'd called Charlie. He was the only

person she could think of who wouldn't automatically kill Chris. Even the angels kept a wary eye on her husband. Rumor was they had orders to step in and kill Chris if he so much as twitched a finger in the direction of world domination, which was better than their previous modus operandi of: kill the Antichrist. Still, this constant watching... *I'll have to do something about it.* She didn't want anything getting in the way, if and when her husband finally fulfilled his destiny.

She'd hoped that having Charlie over would help her find a way to remove the angelic guards. He did, after all, have an in with their boss.

Bad idea. Instead, her ex-beau had deliberately baited her husband, eyeing her in a way that wasn't appropriate with *any* married woman, let alone one married to the Antichrist.

And here she was, alone with her ex, in the kitchen where she'd blindly followed as Charlie fixed himself an ice pack.

"You should go." She slammed the freezer shut, only to have him trap her hand with his.

She stared at his fingers. Tanned. The nails blunt and clean, his skin smooth, not callused. She didn't get the same rush that she always got with Chris.

Charlie, though, felt something he shouldn't. "I never told you... I wish I'd defied my father and called you after that summer."

Because God hadn't approved of his son dating the granddaughter of a sorcerer. Never mind that Elyon had had his son born for his zillionth incarnation into a silver-spoon family that skirted every environmental law it could. *She* was the bad one.

Tugging her hand free, she turned from him. "No point rehashing the past. Truth is, you didn't call, not even when you finally struck out on your own. Not saying that you should have," she hastily added. "Just that it was one summer when we were teenagers." That she'd kind of forgotten.

"One glorious summer," said the guy who seemed determined to rehash the past.

She braced her hands on the counter by the sink as she faced him. "I'm married, Charlie."

"To a man who doesn't appreciate you. Who's off getting drunk by himself."

"Are you telling me you never drink alone?"

"I'm almost never alone."

"That's kind of sad." She wrinkled her nose. "Everyone needs alone time." A chance to get in tune with oneself.

"I want to see you again," he said as she went to the door and opened it, standing to the side, a silent indication that he should leave.

"Still married," she reiterated.

"And if you weren't?"

"That'd better not be an intro to an offer to kill my husband and make me a widow."

"You know how my father feels about murder."

She knew how Elyon felt, but looking at Charlie's

intent gaze, she had to wonder about him. After all, he wasn't the one in charge, making up all the rules. On the contrary, her understanding was that his daddy bent quite a few of them for his errant son. Was murder really out of the realm?

Funny how she'd never entertained these thoughts before. Being with Chris and marinating in his cynicism had her finally seeing other possibilities, hearing the double entendres in people's words.

Jesus as a killer, though? So profane, she just couldn't fathom it.

"I think you should go."

"What of your husband?" Charlie asked.

"You let me worry about my husband."

"I thought you needed help following him."

She did. But not Charlie's help. Calling her ex had been a mistake. Since Uber took too long to arrive, maybe she'd have to bite the bullet and buy some extra wheels. Their budget couldn't handle it, but—

"It worked."

What worked? Then it hit her. The beer, the weed, the deadly combination she'd encouraged all evening long.

She snapped to attention and looked out to where Charlie pointed. The driveway. She could hear the rattle of the garage door.

Chris was on the move.

And Charlie dangled his keys, waiting for an answer.

"I told you, I don't want your help."

"You really shouldn't lie. We both know you can't follow him without me."

The point stung. Probably a bad idea using him as a chauffeur, but more fun than doing kitchen cleanup. Plus, she really needed to know what Chris was up to.

She nodded. "Follow him."

Let's see exactly what you're doing, dear husband. Hopefully nothing that would make her mad enough to become a widow.

6

BAMBI STEPPED out of the cab without bothering to leave a tip. She never had to pay for transport. But she did have to reapply her lipstick.

A succubus never left home without some—or mints for when she went heavy on the garlic. Something her ex-boyfriend Chris—not her brother Chris, but wizard Chris—had never approved of. What did he expect? He was dating a succubus. A pity his poor, fragile human body couldn't handle it.

The breakup had been sad. The rebound sex? Invigorating. And now, she was free to do anyone she pleased. Even cab drivers.

The happy man sped off, and she surveyed her surroundings.

From the outside, the warehouse seemed rather benign. There wasn't any light coming through the blacked-out windows high above. No noise either. The parking lot behind the chain-link fence was mostly empty. No surprise.

People who came to this place rarely left sober. Nor did they leave anything as identifying as a vehicle. Never knew when the joint might get raided. Every so often, the cops happened to get a new gung-ho captain who wouldn't just accept a bribe and turn a blind eye.

Those kinds of altruistic people never lasted too long. Everyone had a weakness.

For many people, it was sex, and Bambi knew all about that. Her hips rolled as she walked, a sensual glide that drew the gaze and kept it.

Only two guys were there to appreciate her moves. The pair—having a cigarette to the side of the entrance —appeared casual. And human. An appearance meant to deceive, but she saw them for what they were. Trolls under glamour, made to look like big men, yet a haze of green clung to them—the magic she could see. If she squinted, she saw past it to the ugliness underneath. Rough, callused skin. Big, sloping foreheads. Greasy hanks of hair. And loincloths that weren't long yet hid them amply. Trolls possessed rather small hands and feet for their size.

But they were male, which meant when Bambi swished her hips, they paid attention.

Troll, human, pygmy dwarf from the South American jungles... Didn't matter. Her succubus nature drew them all. These big doormen were no different.

"I want into the party." She purred the words as she drew near.

"No party here, toots." A rumbly voice. How delightful.

Her pussy quivered at the thought of it rumbling against her. A troll was ugly, but if she turned off the magic of othersight for a few minutes, she could forget it long enough for a snack.

I'm hungry. Her carnal side complained, and this despite its recent meal. She'd have to bite the bullet soon. Imbibe an entire soul in one meal, aspirate the moment of their death in order to sate her succubus side.

A couple of deaths a year to retain control of her herself, with sips in between to tide her over for a while. A smart succubus didn't ignore the warning signs of hunger. Bambi had never forgotten those early years when she let herself go.

I used to have such an insatiable hunger. An addict for sex and souls. She'd managed to fix one of those predilections.

It took meeting the little lamb to turn her life around. Now, she ran several sex addiction therapy groups. They were great for keeping her fed. The strip joint where she worked as a feature dancer paid her bills, though.

"You aren't going to seriously leave me out in the cold." Her lower lip jutted in a pout as she ran her fingernail down the troll's humanish chest.

She saw the troll shiver even if the glamoured version didn't.

"It's summertime. Not cold," declared his partner, not wearing the same lusty gaze. Rather he seemed angry with her because of... Bambi cast a sly glance back at Troll Number One. Heretofore known as Oblivious. And the other, WantsIt.

Easy enough to solve. She lured Oblivious in with sultry lips and a wiggle of her hips. Then managed to draw Wantsit into the equation. Bambi slipped out from between them, leaving them writhing in the alley, doing her part to bring the trolls together, leaving the way into the warehouse clear.

Hiking up her skirt and fluffing her boobs, she entered the building.

A noisy warehouse, as it turned out. The sound-proofing was owed to magic, a heavy shell of it encasing the building. Within, enough cryptids to make a scientist ejaculate without touching himself.

Just about every fable was probably represented in the gathered crowd. From goblin, elf, and fairy to things more exotic and alien. They were seated on hovering discs, raised at different levels all around the large space, the aerial view quite spectacular. On the ground, where the late arrivals clustered, a little harder to see, was the topic of attraction.

Wanting a spot at the front, Bambi began to wiggle her way through the crowd. "Ooh, how did my hand get there?" A firm cup. "Nice package." A slow grind. "I might want to grab your number later."

She tingled all over as she left a trail of horny bodies behind. Reaching the front, she plopped herself onto an available male lap, ignored the screech of his wife, and perused the ring—bound in a shield of magic —before her.

The concrete floor had been carved to form channels, and in those etched lines, they'd poured a silver-titanium mix, an excellent alloy for conducting magic. Used in this manner, it amplified a spell. In this case, a shield.

The magical dome kept the combatants and guts in the middle of the building for the crowd's viewing pleasure.

Leaning forward, the man behind her groaned as his hips ground against her. Someone hit her and demanded she get off.

I'm trying. She had her thighs clamped tight and her vibrating pocket bullet going full tilt inside.

Her orgasm would have to wait, though. Her eyes widened as she grasped what happened inside the ring.

Not what she'd expected.

Definitely not what *he* would want to hear.

And yet, there was her brother, Christopher, floating midair, lobbing magical spears of blue fire while dead bodies grappled with the tail of the giant worm attacking.

And when her brother won? He pounded his chest and screamed, "The Antichrist wins again!"

Again? Then again, she should have known this wasn't the first time he'd participated in some kind of paranormal fight club. The idiot.

She wondered how long he'd known his powers were back. She also wondered why his wife looked so pissed. Isobel stood outside the magical cage, arms crossed and lips pressed into an angry line. *What is she doing with Charlie?*

Handsy cousin, Charlie, who hugged a touch too long, stared just a bit more than he should. But he never crossed that line. Just skirted close.

Charlie stood right behind Isobel. Much too close. If Chris noticed...

Bambi lifted herself abruptly, ignoring the cry of disappointment. Didn't look back at the screamed, "bastard," followed by gunfire.

She kept an eye partially on Chris, who was surrounded by gushing sycophants wearing short skirts and too much makeup.

Wannabe whores. It took work, lots of it—on her back, knees, stomach, suspended, and more—to constantly win the slut-of-the-year award. It wasn't the number of times that counted. It was the quality, too.

Bambi held the record in both.

She slid herself in front of Isobel, blocking her gaze before something unfortunate happened.

"If it isn't my favorite sister-in-law."

"I am your only sister-in-law. What are you doing here, Bambi?"

"Just here for the show, like everyone else."

A reply that caused Isobel's gaze to narrow. "So you admit you knew about Chris's extracurricular activities?"

"Me?" Bambi feigned shock. "I am just as surprised as you are. I came here on the recommendation of a friend. I never expected to see my brother. What is Chris doing here?"

Isobel's shoulders rolled. "No idea."

"And what are you doing with *him*?" She didn't hide her disdain.

Charlie managed a pleasant reply. "Bambi, lovely to see you, dear cousin."

"Is it?" Turning to Isobel, she added, "You shouldn't be here with Charlie."

"My place is with my husband."

"Are you sure that is your husband in the ring?" Bambi asked in all seriousness. Because the Chris she knew didn't have the skill to float midair and throw magic missiles. *And the Devil won't be happy about this development.*

Isobel's lips flattened. "He's not possessed. Just stressed."

"He's using zombies to play fight club."

"Honing his skills in a safe environment is not a crime." Isobel's chin tilted.

"Making himself appear dangerous and possibly

looking to fulfill his destiny of becoming the ruler of Hell might not be the best idea."

"Let Lucifer try and kill him. Chris can handle it."

"I wasn't talking about Lucifer. Gaia has been a little crazy lately. The Earth keeps rumbling because of it." Bambi had heard of pregnancy hormones, but a goddess, especially one as powerful of Gaia, in the grips of it made her want to check out Limbo for a while. Leave on an extended trip.

"What's Mother Earth got to do with my husband?"

"She's pregnant."

"And?"

"With a boy."

"Chris isn't going to kill a baby," Isobel scoffed.

"Then who is he planning to kill?" Bambi asked. "Because that is combat magic." She jabbed a finger over her shoulder.

"Just because he's practicing doesn't mean he's planning to use it for nefarious purposes."

"So what if he is?" Charlie interjected. "Really, dear cousin, you can't expect someone like Chris to just sit around at home, twiddling his thumbs. The man has a destiny, and that calling doesn't involve doing nothing."

"This is far from nothing. He needs a different hobby," Bambi insisted. "We can't keep hiding him forever."

"We?" Isobel homed in on the word. "Who's been hiding him?"

Did Isobel really not know? Had Lucifer not told them about the spell he cast?

Of course, he didn't. Father thrives on secrets. "Ever since the wedding, Lucifer has been hiding my brother from Chris's mother. A good thing, too, since the last seal on her prison broke." A chill wind blew through the building, and everyone shivered.

"She escaped?" Charlie asked.

"Duh," Bambi said with a roll of her eyes. "The door opened. Of course, she fled her prison. And the moment she did, Father doubled down on his spell so she couldn't find Chris—or Isobel for that matter."

"Lucifer knows where she is?" Charlie asked.

A roll of Bambi's shoulders undulated her entire body. "If he does, then he hasn't told me."

"Then how does he know for sure she escaped?"

"Dunno. I didn't feel it, but Lucifer said the moment she exited her prison it was as if reality wobbled for a minute. Good thing he already had a shield over Chris, or she would have probably made a beeline for him."

Isobel frowned. "Wait a second, when you say shield..." She looked away from Bambi to the ring. "Your dad is the reason Chris's magic doesn't work. He did it on purpose to suppress it."

"He did it to protect him," Bambi said, only partially lying.

"Protect, my ass," Isobel exclaimed. "By nullifying Chris's abilities, Lucifer rendered a threat to his crown impotent. That's low, even for the Devil."

"Suppressing his magic was a better option than killing him." Which was what some of Lucifer's advisers had encouraged him to do.

"Does it never occur to anyone to treat Chris like an adult? To let him make his own choices?" Isobel took her husband's side.

"His decisions could end the world." Which, personally, Bambi didn't care about. There were places other than these that a succubus could live and feed.

"Is that why you're here? To convince him to stop using his magic?" Isobel kept hammering.

"I'm here because Lucifer ordered it." And one didn't say no to the Devil.

"Go back to your father and tell him to leave Chris alone. He needs to stop meddling. Take off the shield. Chris is going crazy thinking he can't do magic."

"He seems to be doing magic fine right now," Charlie pointed out, rejoining the conversation.

"Which is a problem," Bambi remarked. "He shouldn't be able to do it at all."

"But he is. Because he is obviously stronger than you believe. At least when drunk." Charlie, still not helping.

Bambi glared at him. "I still don't understand why you're here."

"Because he, unlike a certain sister-in-law of mine,

offered to help me with my poor husband."

"Poor?" Bambi waved a hand. "He's fighting off a tremor worm and ogres like a pro."

Isobel leaned around Bambi and glared at the ring. "I'm well aware he's lobbing magic and ordering around the dead as if it's easy. We will be talking about that."

"I'd think you'd want to talk to him more about those women of loose morals he's hanging with," Charlie the shit disturber added.

"Chris wouldn't cheat on me," Isobel stated with firm conviction.

"Don't be so sure of that," whispered a voice. From behind Bambi—who never sensed a thing—stepped Famine, one of the four horsemen.

Unlike the last time she'd seen the male, he seemed well fed, his jowls not hanging slackly now, his suit fitting his corpulent body like a second skin.

Someone was obviously not lacking for sustenance.

"What are you doing here?" snapped Isobel. "I thought Chris told you never to bother him again."

"Who says I'm *bothering* him? I am just a bystander, feeding on the greed of the crowd. The hope they will win. The dejection when they don't. Absolutely delicious."

The more Famine spoke, the more Bambi did her best not to fidget or worry about her makeup. She kept fit enough to fight off that pesky cellulite, but she could do nothing about her age. Getting old. Soon, she wouldn't be able to keep up with today's younger whores. Someone would shove her out of the limelight and take over her spot on the bed, legs spread.

Sob.

Slap. The crack of Isobel's palm across Famine's cheek caused him to yelp. The confidence he'd starved from her began seeping back.

"You stop that, right now," Isobel demanded. "Leave Bambi alone."

Mind clear again, Bambi gaped at the horseman who'd done his best to feed on her insecurities. He had a lot in common with his sister, Pestilence.

"Insolent, bitch. You should be on your knees groveling to me," hissed Famine.

"The only man I worship is my husband."

"Says the woman who's here with her lover." Famine looked past her to smirk at Charlie. "Maybe I should regurgitate a bit of my meal and feed your husband's jealousy."

Before Bambi could react and stop Famine from acting, he shoved her aside. A piercing whistle cut through all sound. Drew all eyes. Including Chris's.

His gaze widened as he beheld his wife.

Narrowed when he saw who stood behind her.

Chris didn't need Pestilence to poison his mind. Jealousy was a powerful beast all on its own, and when Charlie stupidly put his hand on Isobel's arm while murmuring, "maybe we should leave," Bambi's brother snapped.

7

"CHARLIE, you idiot. Get away from me." Isobel warned him a moment too late.

Then again, it was probably too late the moment she stepped into the warehouse with another man.

The good news? *Chris would never hurt me.*

But Charlie?

Yeah. The blue fireballs streaked fast and furious, hitting the shield. A force field that rang like a discordant bell as it tried to contain all that violent magic.

"Oh, fuck," Bambi breathed. "Now you've done it."

But Famine wasn't there to listen, having slipped off into the crowd, feeding on their excitement.

Did the idiots not realize the danger?

Magic kept striking the shield, and Charlie still stupidly held her arm. He tugged her. "Come on, Isobel. I'll get us out of here."

Except leaving now with Charlie would only make

things worse. The man inside the dome, the man with the glowing red eyes, would think she'd abandoned him for another.

Rather than move away, she moved toward the shield and placed her hands on it, the strangely spongy surface fogging and heating at her touch.

On the other side, her husband approached. His eyes lost their red glow and turned into black pools of darkness, his body vibrating with power. So much power.

Not all his.

Isobel knew the feeling of Chris's magic. The darkness emanating from him right now?

Looked as if Mommy had found her baby.

The realization had Isobel stepping back from the shield. Yet Chris still approached. His hands lifted, glowing, the palms pressing against the invisible dome containing him and his miniature army of the dead.

The shield disintegrated, leaving nothing between the crowd and the man possessed by the dark deity inside.

The spectators hushed for a second then cheered. Idiots.

Did they not realize the danger?

Chris lifted his hand, a ball of blue fire sitting on the palm. Very pretty. Extremely deadly.

He stared at her. Through her.

The chill running through her veins a reminder that it wasn't her husband driving the body.

Still, she tried to reason. "Chris, honey, maybe you should put that fireball away?"

The head cocked. The lips twisted into a sneer.

"No." He lobbed it, and it singed past her, close enough that she wondered if he'd missed.

A glance over her shoulder, though, showed the real target. The magical fire chased Charlie, who weaved through the crowd. A gathering that bellowed, finally realizing the danger. Too late. Some stood in the way and died as the magical fire burned through them. Fresh souls for Hell.

Bambi had hit the floor the moment the shield dropped and now tugged a gaping Isobel down to join her.

"We have to stop him," Bambi remarked, lying low and watching her brother, who ignored them both to stalk after Charlie.

"I am not hurting Chris."

"Not Chris. Him." Bambi pointed to Famine, who cackled off to the side as he fed more insecurities to Chris then gorged on the resulting rage.

"Kill a horseman. Got it." Isobel's hand went to her hip, where she kept her sword. Her handy-dandy magical sword, invisible until she drew it forth. A gift from her dead father.

"You distract Famine, and I'll handle Chris," Bambi suggested.

"Make sure you handle those sluts, too." Because Isobel didn't have time to kill a horseman of the apocalypse and the whores sniffing around her husband. Jealousy wasn't a one-way street.

"On it."

They bumped fists and went to their tasks, Bambi dodging screaming people—some on fire, running rampant—trying to reach her brother, and Isobel to chase after...what was a horseman exactly? Not quite a god, yet impossible thus far to kill.

But it didn't hurt to keep trying. As soon as she came within reach, she slashed her sword and managed a thin slice in his sleeve.

Famine stopped chanting long enough to glare. "You dare to strike me, little girl? Don't you know you can't win? You're nothing but a weaker, paler version of your sister. The runt of the family litter. Poor little Isobel with no magic."

"You lie." Isobel didn't let him feed her insecurity. She didn't let him eat her confidence. She held her head high because she knew the truth. She had magic. It was just different than everyone else's.

She sliced again with her sword, and Famine danced back, avoiding the sharp tip. Maybe he could be harmed.

Harrying him, she pushed him into the ring, empty of Chris and his sister. The pair of them had disappeared.

But that didn't stop Isobel from pursuing the horseman that would rob her of all hope, the being who would feast on her confidence. She wasn't a buffet for his perverted magic. She kept jabbing and slicing. From the stands, another voice called out, a feminine one.

"You were never your mother's favorite." Pestilence had arrived, her white hair and dress barely hinting of green. She'd not yet recovered from her previous encounter with Chris outside the crypt when they'd gone looking for Isobel's father. Months ago now, and yet it appeared the poisoner of minds was still weakened. Or Isobel had gotten stronger because the doubts barely tickled. Perhaps Isobel wasn't Mama's favorite, but she was her papa's little girl.

Lunge, parry, dice. A streak of oozing gray from Famine's arm. It steamed in the air.

"You're a meaningless cog in the grand scheme," Pestilence hissed. "The Son of Perdition doesn't need you at all."

"No, he doesn't, which is why we work well together." They were partners.

"He could do so much better."

"But he chose me." Chris had chosen Isobel to be his wife.

"You're fat."

Isobel smiled as Famine found himself with his back against the wall. "I'm just right." She lunged forward, and her sword slid between his ribs, right into where a human heart might be.

Except he wasn't human. His body dissolved into a gray fog that steamed a final scream. "This isn't over."

It was for today.

She turned to face Pestilence and waggled her sword in the other horseman's direction.

Her features pinched, the female sketched a portal, but before she used it, Pestilence uttered one last poisonous whisper, "You'll never win."

Funny, because I just did.

However, winning a small skirmish didn't help Isobel find her husband. He'd disappeared with Bambi. Where?

She fired off a text to her sister-in-law—just three letters: *WTF?*. And got one in reply.

All is good. Sleeping it off. Will bring him by in the morning.

Bring him where? To their house, a plain old dwelling that lacked any kind of protective spells? It wouldn't stop a horseman. Heck, it couldn't even keep out mice.

But where else could she go?

Another text hit her phone, this time from her mother. *I need you. Can you stay at the house for a few days?*

How propitious. Her family home was the perfect place for them to regroup.

But Chris would never agree. He had too much pride.

Which was why she planned to use it against him.

8

Sunlight filled the garden, a bright puddle of brilliance illuminating the shadows, enhancing the vibrant greenery all around.

In the center of the lushness sat a table with two chairs, the ornate metal kind, painted white. Sitting at the table, an elegant woman with her blouse buttoned high on her neck, and her skirt long enough that even sitting he didn't see her ankles. Gray hair was coiled at her nape.

He peered around. "Where am I?"

"The hanging gardens of Babylonia. I helped design them, you know. Not that anyone ever gave me credit." The woman's voice was monotone even if her words expressed disgruntlement.

"Who are you?" Chris took a step forward, prickled by curiosity.

"What a silly question, child. Who do you think I am?"

He could think of one person, but he'd never seen her face. Never actually met her. "It can't be you."

"Don't speak to me of can't. There is no such thing as can't. Sit down."

Chris stood still. At least, he meant to. His body, however, moved on its own, sliding him forward to the chair and bending him enough that his butt hit the wrought-iron seat.

Dark eyes perused him. "Well, who am I?"

"Mother?" The query emerged from him as he stared right back. Surely, this elegant woman wasn't the monstrous thing that used dead body parts to form a mega creature. Not the entity that had possessed his foster mother and chased him through prison.

Her lips pursed. "Yes, I am your mother, the one who birthed your fourteen-pound body. Your head was the worst. Absolutely melon-sized. Still is, I see. You always were a bit large up there. Not sure if it made you any smarter." She eyed him, and he gaped.

"Aren't you supposed to be in prison?"

"Are you speaking of the prison my son never visited?"

"I didn't know about you."

"You do now, and yet still no attempt to see me."

"You want me to visit?" His brow creased.

The woman poured from a teapot he only just

noticed. "Of course, I would have liked a visit. A card would have even sufficed."

He managed to retort, "Says the woman who never sent me shit."

"I sent you plenty. Did that despicable Clarice never give my gifts to you?"

"I never got anything." That he knew of.

His mother tsked. A real tsk. Rather fascinating. Growing up, his mom, Clarice, had never rebuked him. When he misbehaved, he was simply practicing for his Antichrist destiny.

"Where are we?" he asked. This entire place and conversation had a dreamlike quality to it.

"I told you, the hanging gardens of Babylonia."

"But how? How did I get here?"

"Are you so behind in your education that you never learned even the simplest things?"

"I was raised by humans. What did you expect?" And only until his teens. Then, after his adopted mom had gotten arrested for murder, he did his best to avoid getting beaten too badly in his foster homes.

"Raised by humans, only a step above the beasts in this world. That is the fault of your father."

"Dad is a dick."

"Language."

Rap. Despite there being none present, he could feel the slap of a ruler across his hand. And, yes, he knew what that felt like. Not because a teacher had ever done that to him, but more because, as a kid, it was the type of game boys played. The object being: don't flinch, and most definitely never cry.

Had his mother seriously tried to punish him? "This is my dream. I'll talk whatever damn way I please."

Slap. Tap. More raps over his knuckles, harder this time. He clenched his teeth lest he suck in a breath.

"Oooh, do it harder. That tickles," he lied.

"If this is your way of ingratiating yourself to me, it's failing."

"Your motherly instinct leaves much to be desired."

"Perhaps I'd be more inspired if you weren't such a disappointment." Her lips turned down.

"If I'm such a failure, then why are you here?" Other than to prey on his obvious insecurities.

"You're making a mistake."

"Story of my life."

"Bad enough you married *that girl.*" Said with utmost disapproval. "I need you to stay out of Hell politics."

Since he had no idea what she spoke of, he could have easily given in to her request. However, Chris was ever the ornery sort. "Hell is my inheritance."

"You will take nothing from the Devil," she stated, holding out a plate of scones. "Even if he offers it."

"You can't tell me what to do."

"Are you so sure about that? I can do more than you realize, son. Who do you think rides your body when you black out? Haven't you thought to ask yourself what's happening while I'm distracting you in here?" Her lips split into a wide smile. Give her a balloon, and she'd have been a perfect girlfriend for a certain psychotic clown.

"Give me back my body." He looked at the half-drunk tea in his hand and cursed. "Have you been drugging me?"

"I don't have to when you do such a fine job yourself."

"Get out of my head."

"I'm not in your head. We're in—"

"—the hanging garden, or at least a dream version of it. Yeah. I get it. Which means I can get out of here by waking up." He glanced around at the perfect blue sky, the expertly groomed foliage. Everything just right. All fucking fake.

"This isn't real," he muttered, clenching his fists by his sides.

"Really, son, that's the kind of thing a child says. You're a demi-god. Use that power."

"I can't."

"You've been made to think you can't. Try again."

He shoved away from the table, rising angrily to his feet. "You think I haven't tried? I try to access my magic every single fucking day. But I can't. It's not there."

"It's there," she said, her lip curling in disdain. "Obviously, you're just too weak to figure it out."

"Why do you care? Hunh? Why is it so important

to you that I access my magic? I'll tell you why," he yelled before she could reply. "Because you're planning something."

"Of course I am planning, because not all of us are complacent sheep, content with our lot in life."

"Who says I'm content?"

"Then fight for it. Fight for your heritage. You are descended from the Branch of the Terrible Ones. The Son of Perdition. Show. Me. Your. Strength." The last words roared out of his mother, and with each syllable, the sunny sky darkened, clouds boiled, lightning flashed, and the thunder boomed, shaking the ground.

His mother stood in the tempest she'd called, untouched by it. Must be nice. He, on the other hand, felt every bite of the wind as it tore at his clothes and ripped at his hair. He felt the dark chill of the unnatural storm.

But the storm wasn't the most dangerous thing. Riding a bolt of lightning came War, his mighty red steed no longer as gaunt as it had been, its eyes blazing with baleful fire. Atop the horse, War's rusty-colored armor gleamed, and the lance he held was raised just high enough to impale the idiot gaping at him.

Chris threw himself to the side as the horseman of the apocalypse thundered past him. Hitting the dirt face-first, Chris should have felt fear. Instead...

"Motherfucker!" Because what else would those two have been doing the entire time they were locked in that prison dimension? Chris rose to his feet and huffed, hot breaths that steamed in the cold air.

His rigid body faced War, who'd pivoted his horse around and pranced in place, preparing for his next charge.

Arms hanging loosely by his sides, Chris watched War through a hank of hair. His fists clenched.

"Armies of the dead, I call you to my banner." A pole suddenly appeared in War's free hand. Atop it fluttered a tattered flag that bore a symbol. The same squiggle that was on his ass. χιϛ. An ancient way of saying 666.

My symbol.

And to that banner flocked the dead, rising from the earth, their decayed fingers poking first as they clawed themselves from the grave until they stood behind War.

That's my army.

Mine...

The susurration of his mother reached him, a whisper through the tempest. "Yes, yours, my son. Call them to you. Make them obey their true master."

Rather than tell her to fuck off, he reached inside for the magic. Reached deep, expecting to find a cold, empty well. Instead...

He gasped aloud in delight as it filled him. Lovely power, strength to do it all. To order the army to, "Tickle War until he cries uncle."

Dead fingers reached for the red warrior, who

slashed at them with his sword before dashing away on his mighty steed, all while Chris's mother applauded. "About time you took control of your power again."

"Speaking of control…"

With the magic flowing through him, he now had the strength to cast aside this dream. "A la shazam cheese and pickle sandwich," he yelled. The world around him twisted and—

He awoke with a mouthful of dirt. Since this was a familiar experience, he didn't immediately spit it out and let anyone know he'd woken. Not until he assessed the situation better.

First, he took stock of his body. Toe wiggle? Check. Arm jiggle, finger twitch. Check and check. Crack open one eye, up close encounter with stubby grass and soil. Not a prison cell or the dump or Hell or some other nasty place. Also, it wasn't his bed or his house, which meant another blackout.

But on the good news front? Still alive. Seemingly unbroken. Oddly craving a cup of tea and…

He blinked. He felt as if something hovered just out of reach, a feeling of sunshine and the smell of baked goods.

Which was completely opposite to the face full of dirt and drizzle of rain on his back. *Where am I?* He stretched his mind back to the last thing he recalled.

Roast beef dinner—so fucking delicious. Beers, a lot of them. His cousin Jesus, a cool fellow. Smoking some epic weed in the backyard. Then…nothing.

What happened? Accidentally spoken aloud.

"What happened," declared a sultry female voice, "is that you've been avoiding me, little brother. Not to mention you've been getting into trouble."

"Trouble is my middle name."

"No, it's not. *Percy.*" Said with a snicker by his sister, Bambi.

"It's a wonder you get any action given you're so good at deflating a man's ego."

"I'll deflate you for pulling that stunt."

"What stunt?" Being prone on his belly, he had to turn his head fully sideways in order to admire the stiletto heels at an impossible height, arching his sister's feet into a surely excruciating angle. "Why are you here, and while we're at it, where is here?"

"As if you don't know." She crouched down but thankfully kept her knees pressed together. Some things a brother should never see.

"Let's pretend I don't know where I am. Enlighten me."

"We are in your graveyard about fifty yards outside that remodeled church you call home."

"In my yard?" His extended cemetery yard. He rolled onto his back and noted the cloudy skies overhead. What time was it? "How did I get here?"

"Epic bar hop."

"Really?" He didn't recall but still smiled. "Cool. Is that why you're here then, to give me shit for having a good time?"

"No, I'm here because the damned departed want you to stop playing with their bodies."

"I am not into necrophilia, no matter what my biology teacher said I did with that skull."

"Don't you pretend like you aren't, little brother. I know what you did with those bodies." Bambi stood and managed to tower over him with a disapproving air.

Bad enough he had to deal with that kind of shit from his wife, he wasn't taking it from his sister, too. He scrambled to his feet. "I didn't do nothing because it wasn't me."

"Liar, liar, pants on fire." She tossed her head, and pursed her pouty lips while wagging a finger at him. Bambi was all about the act. Even this early in the morning, she looked slutty—which those who knew her would realize was the utmost compliment—in a furry mauve bolero atop a curve-hugging dress that barely covered her cooch.

On anyone else, especially Isobel, he would have drooled, but on his sister, he winced. "Dammit, sis, put some damned clothes on. You're making me cold looking at you."

"Prude. I swear, sometimes you have more in common with our uncle."

"Speaking of whom, I met his son."

"Charlie?" Her voice lilted. "Well, I'll bet that was a treat."

"I rather liked him."

"Of course, you did. I'm sure he was nice to you."

"Nice?" He wouldn't have said that, not with Charlie's sense of humor. But then again, what did he know?

"Surprised you had him over given your jealousy issues."

"What are you talking about?" Then it hit him. The memory of certain words returned. "Isobel used to date Jesus," he blurted, and the anger hit him at the same time. He whirled and threw a fist, the crack of his knuckles on stone enough to draw a sharp gasp from him.

"Temper, temper," chided his sister. "She might have dated him, but she never fucked him, even if he says otherwise. Hard to believe he is related to Elyon given his mouthy ways."

"Are you implying he talked trash about Isobel?"

"Not implying, stating. He bragged to everyone he could about shagging Rasputin's granddaughter. Which we know is a lie. Isobel was a virgin when you married her."

That fact was the only thing that didn't send him off into a blind rage. "How is it Jesus can lie?"

"Because he never actually said anything."

The statement confused him. "Hold on, if he never said anything, then how did he brag?"

"People made assumptions. He didn't correct them. Never said a word. Which is how he keeps himself free of most sin. He lets others do his dirty work."

"Does Isobel know this about him?"

"Everyone with half a brain cell who meets him notices it."

"If he's a passive-aggressive douchetard, then why did she invite him into my house?"

"One of two reasons I'd guess, starting with she genuinely wants to find you more family to bond with."

"I have you," Chris stated.

"Gee, don't I feel all soft and mushy inside."

He crossed his arms and moped. "You should. I wanted to be an only child."

Bambi laughed. "And here I always wished for a cute younger brother I could boss around."

"You said there were two reasons Isobel might have invited Jesus. What's the other one?"

"Why, to shove it in Charlie's face that she married his nemesis."

"Well, that backfired. He and I decided not to be enemies." One of the few things he was certain of regarding the previous night.

"Ah, how cute. You and your cousin bonded."

"As common allies, not family."

"I guess it didn't last that long since, last I saw, Charlie was running from you because you were trying to kill him."

"I tried to kill Jesus fucking Christ?" Just how drunk and high had he gotten after dinner?

"Don't worry, you failed. But that's not why I came. You've got to stop raising the dead."

"What are you talking about?"

"You." She jabbed a finger at him. "Dead people." Aimed at the ground. "Stop."

"Hate to break it to you, sis, but I can't raise them anymore. Haven't since the wedding."

"Yes, you have," stated Bambi with firm certainty.

"No, I haven't. You think I haven't tried?" Every day for the past month he'd been out there calling to the bones under the ground. To no avail.

"Why are you lying?"

"About?"

"I was there last night. I saw what you did."

"Isn't that the title of a movie?"

Bambi grabbed him by the ear, and like many a boy —and man—before him, Chris yelped and followed where she yanked. Because it fucking hurt.

"Let go of my ear."

"No."

"You can't treat me like this. I'm the bloody Antichrist."

"Right now, you're just my sodding hung-over brother who is pissing off damned souls who don't deserve it because he's got Mommy issues and he's only able to deal with them in a violent fashion using other people's body parts!" she shouted.

More spectacular than the fact that he'd managed to make Bambi blow her top was what she said.

EVE LANGLAIS

"I do not have Mommy issues."

"Oh, please. 'My mommy left me, and my daddy was never around, so I'm going to act out until one of them pays me attention.' Did it ever occur to you that Daddy is watching? He just doesn't have time to pat you on the back and tell you you'll never live up to expectations."

"He watches me?"

"He watches everyone. It's his job. But he especially keeps an eye on his kids. Mostly because he fears them backstabbing him in rebellion, but..." Bambi shrugged. "In his defense, he's had sons before who tried to kill him."

"What of his daughters?"

Bambi smirked. "He dotes on us. Why would we hurt him?"

"He's an asshole."

"He's Daddy."

And with that, he knew he couldn't count on Bambi to help him if—no, make that *when*—he went after his dad.

"Change of subject." Since Daddy was a sore one. "What exactly have I been doing while drunk?" The events that left him covered in dirt and other things. He plucked a hunk of desiccated scalp from his shirt and dropped it to the ground.

"You seriously don't remember?" Bambi eyed him and then whistled. "Goodness gracious to Betsy, that whore in garters, you really don't recall, do you?"

Bambi laughed, a rich sound that caused a few heads to turn in disapproval, early mourners come to pay respects.

"I keep saying I don't. What's the scoop?" They walked away from the visitors towards the road, where she'd parked.

"I can do better than tell you. I can show you. Get in." By in she meant her car, a little red number, two doors, low to the ground, and capable of Mach 3.

"My house is right here." The wicker hanging chair on the front porch called to his aching body. He didn't ignore it. He left his sister on the sidewalk so that he might collapse in his chair. He spun in half circles a few times and blamed that for feeling dizzy when he grabbed the phone thrust at him and began to watch the video.

"What is this?" he asked, even if he could see.

"It's you. And no, it wasn't me who took the footage, but someone in the audience. This is from last week, apparently."

The words, "it can't be," hovered on the tip of his tongue, but ultimately remained unspoken because it was him. While the video itself jiggled as the person holding it got jostled, he didn't have a problem deciphering what he saw.

Standing tall in a clearing bound by glowing silver lines on the floor was Chris. Chris—or at least his twin wearing the same clothes, albeit cleaner—his expression blank. And arrayed at his back, the dead. The fresh ones at the back, the more decayed taking up the area at the front. The zombies, while cool, were only a distraction to tire his opponent. A troll with a few ogres as his backup. Once that video finished, she loaded another.

"This is the fight from last night."

He felt a little bit like Kevin Bacon in *Tremors* as the giant worm reared its ugly head and opened a maw full of jagged teeth. Chris sat riveted and watched as he launched his army of the undead and his hands moved in complex patterns, throwing magic. And, oh yeah, he floated.

"Is that really me?" Because the guy in the video was badass. A true mage and fighter.

"It's you. According to a security guard I talked to, you show up at random, asking to be pitted against the toughest they have to offer."

"What is this, like a fight club?"

"An underground one for non-humans."

"How did I find it?" Because he sure as hell didn't have the slightest clue where he'd go about getting an invite to a secret underground club. Kind of cool, though.

Rather than reply, Bambi questioned, "How come you didn't tell me you could wield your magic again?"

"Because I can't. At least not once I've sobered up." He stared at his hands. Working hands, the dirt creased in the calluses. "I can't feel the power at all."

"Obviously, you can. Or do you need to watch the video again?"

He'd watch it again. Just because he looked damned slick!

He forwarded himself a copy to his mailbox then handed Bambi's phone back. Leaving his fingers empty, drumming on the edge of the chair. He no longer felt like spinning. Especially since his world was tilting already.

"How come I can't remember?"

"Are you sure you can't?" she asked. "Maybe it feels like a dream?"

"I don't dream." *Most especially not of gardens*, a random thought that made him frown. "Since you're here, I'm going to guess Dad is pissed I've been raising the dead."

"A little. Lucky for you, he's still strutting because of his marriage to Mother Nature. You missed a beautiful wedding, by the way."

"I was busy. Work." Car accident. Entire family gone in one fell swoop.

"I take it you heard the news?"

He didn't bother playing dumb. "You mean that dear old Dad managed to strike gold with one of his swimmers? Yeah." Gaia was pregnant. With a boy. Yet another person to supplant him.

Pregnancies are fragile things.

Surely, it wasn't his mind that whispered that?

"Dad's pretty stoked."

"What happened to killing sons before birth and all that crap because of prophecy?" Because Lucifer didn't allow his boys to live, not when all the seers claimed the Antichrist was destined to rule Hell.

I am the Antichrist. For now. What happened when the baby was born and there were two? Would a paradox occur, forcing one of them to die?

Sitting on his front porch as dawn crested the horizon with bright rays, he looked out at the deep front yard. Lush, green grass that took him a whole afternoon each week to groom with a push mower and weed whacker.

But it wasn't as bad as the care and upkeep of the older home, finished in stone where the old church was originally built, with the newer addition covered in wood siding painted a pale blue. The swing he sat on was on a wide porch that wrapped around the entire house. From his spot in the chair swing, he could see a window laced with curtains and, beyond that, the top of his suitcase peeking from the bushes.

What the hell?

He swung out of the chair and stomped for a closer look. Definitely his suitcase. He yanked it free of the bushes and unzipped it. He peeked inside and spotted his things.

"Isobel!" He roared her name as he went to the door. It didn't budge when he turned the knob. He pounded on it.

It remained shut. "Isobel! Let me in. What's going on?"

Silence greeted him.

He hit it again, but the solid door and frame didn't give. Nor did his wife come to reply. The suitcase on the ground mocked him.

"She did not throw me out," he muttered, stalking around to the side.

"She might have, considering what she saw last night," Bambi muttered.

He shot a glare at her. "Who saw what?"

"Isobel. Your wife. I ran into her around the time those groupies started screaming for you."

"Groupies?" He had groupies? And couldn't remember them!

"I am going to go out on a limb and say she heard the ladies propositioning you."

"But I'm married." A dumb reply but the only one he could think of.

"Which only increases your appeal."

A disturbing thought came to him. "I didn't take anyone up on their offer, did I?" Because that might be grounds for a suitcase left outside.

"Are you asking me if you cheated? Not that I saw last night, but it doesn't matter if you did or not where jealousy is concerned."

"I didn't do anything wrong."

"Says you, but let's say we reverse the roles, and

about twenty guys started offering to lick your wife until she came, then fuck her—"

The mere thought of men looking, asking, trying to touch Isobel raised his ire. Fire bubbled inside as he yelled, "Enough!" And still, he couldn't stop the images. The back door to the house blew apart, splinters of wood deflected by an impromptu shield.

Bambi blinked long, mascaraed lashes at him. "Oooh, I bet you get in trouble for that."

He was past giving a shit. Where was his wife? He strode into their home and noted the empty kitchen, the sink bare of dishes, not even the hint of coffee perfuming the air.

The living room lay silent, the television—a splurged-on fifty-inch flat screen—dark. The stairs creaked as he took them two at a time to the second floor. A peek in the master bedroom and bath showed them empty as well, the sheets to the bed still tucked in tightly.

She hadn't slept here last night, so where the fuck was she?

Probably off with that do-gooder, Jesus. The moment he had the thought, he cast it aside. His cousin wouldn't put the moves on his wife. He was Jesus fucking Christ, not some horndog running around seducing married women.

If he applied rational thought to the situation rather than knee-jerk reactions, there were two possibilities.

The first, foul play. If she'd followed him, and to what sounded like a rather disreputable locale, then perhaps she'd run into something she couldn't handle. A kidnapping for ransom, an auctioning of her flesh because she was so beautiful, perhaps even a robbery-murder scenario.

All unacceptable and unlikely because of the damned suitcase, which she'd obviously packed.

Which left him with the other possibility, the one that had him grumbling—and his blood running cold—as he instructed his sister where to drive. Because if Isobel had left, then there was only one place she'd go, one destination he dreaded even more than Hell. Where she'd run if she had a problem.

His in-laws' house—dun-dun-dun...

9

THE MAGIC IMBUING the Rasputin property made Bambi's nipples hard. Always a sure indication that she didn't belong anywhere near this place, no matter how many times the elderly Rasputin leered at her and asked if she wanted to see the etchings in his office.

Drawing her sports car to a stop in front of the mansion, she grimaced. "You sure you want me to leave you here?" Not the first time she'd asked on the drive over. But Chris would not be dissuaded.

"My wife is here," Chris declared, and off he stalked. She watched as he banged on the door and came face-to-face with Isobel. Chris began to argue on the front stoop with his wife. At least Bambi wasn't the cause of the strife for once.

Since he was busy, and she had better things to do, Bambi didn't stick around. She sped out of there. After a night following her brother as he ambled the city on foot, an army of the dead—mostly rats and feline road-kill—trailing him like he was the Pied Piper, she could use a change of scenery.

The road past the gates stretched beautiful and wide, perfect to put the pedal to the metal and, if she were lucky, get pulled over by an officer of the law. She was wearing her good bra today and could use a morning snack. Except from one moment to the next, the road turned from sun-filled asphalt to rutted, red-and-gray, packed dirt, the air full of sifting ash.

The automated wipers swiped at the dust, and she cursed. Brought to Hell in her cute car. Dammit. The last time it had taken three cleanings to get all the flaky stuff out of the leather seats, and she'd had to get the carburetor cleaned.

She braked and waited. Only one person had the power to portal something as big as her vehicle.

Sure enough, the passenger side door opened, and her father—who preferred to be called the Dark Lord—slid into the seat.

"Nice wheels."

Only the best, given the man who'd kept her as a mistress for a month, thought it prudent to gift it to her so that his wife wouldn't find out about their affair.

"You didn't call me here to discuss the merits of the engine under the hood. What's wrong?"

"Wrong? Does anything have to be wrong for a father to want to see his daughter?" Lucifer asked, failing at looking guileless.

Bambi cast him a side-eye. "The only time you pull this kind of stunt is when you want something. Don't beat around the bush. Spit it out."

"My wife has no bush." He leered.

"Are we going to trade dirty jokes all day or get to the point?"

"Gaia is pregnant."

"I know."

"With a son."

"Having second thoughts about it?"

"Not exactly."

"Which means, what?"

"It occurs to me that, given my busy work schedule, I've not spent much time with any of my progeny."

"Usually because you wanted that as an excuse to avoid child support."

"Gaia has insisted I be involved with this pregnancy and child."

"The horror," Bambi said dryly.

"You understand," Lucifer exclaimed with relief. "But here's the thing, I am a busy man. Sin is booming. The new souls coming in daily are more than Hell can handle right now."

"Hire more staff then?"

"And become efficient?" He gasped. "Perish the thought. Never. However, while I am doing an admirable job of slacking and delaying the signing of documents for assignments, I am getting too far behind. There's a backlog in the system, and because the rules,"—a complex set of regulations that Lucifer abided by—"state that delays are to be taken off any declared punishment, I'm losing out."

"You mean, the damned souls are getting credit for time served."

"Exactly. Totally unacceptable. I need to speed up the process while not actually doing more work."

"Like I said, get an assistant."

"I can't hire just anybody. The ruling on souls and their punishments is a tremendously important task. Only a true Baphomet should make those decisions."

Oh, my goodness, this was the moment Bambi had been waiting for her whole life. When her father finally trusted her with more important things than seduction for information or as a messenger-slash-babysitter for her sister.

Lucifer rubbed his chin. "Thinking of asking Muriel to give me a hand."

Nope. Once again, little lamb was his favorite child. "Muri might be a little too busy to help out. And don't forget what happened during your little problem." Namely, the months he'd spent as goody-two-shoes Lucifer because of a spell. Muriel had tried to do his job. Failed. Went on a killing spree. Cried a lot. Everyone in Hell breathed a sigh of relief when the true Dark Lord returned, and Muri quit.

"She would have some help from me. Not much, mind you. I did promise the little lady I'd be around more. Maybe even take a trip. She's been talking about a water birth in some ocean in another dimension."

"You could ask Chris to give you a hand."

"That good-for-nothing wastrel?" The disdain spat from him.

"That good-for-nothing is your son, and he's wasting his life as a grave digger on Earth."

"Asking him to help out, though? Might as well just bare my throat that he might kill me and take over my kingdom. Never!"

"Then suffer. Because you and I both know there's no one else who can help you."

"Aren't you going to suggest yourself?" he asked slyly.

"Not a chance. I've seen what the job did to your looks." She fluffed her hair. "I'll take pole dancing over pushing paper any day."

Lucifer grimaced. "Why did we let the population grow out of control? What happened to full-scale famine, flooding—heck, even a plague—to scale back the numbers?"

"You complained then, too. It took you years to process the last major skirmish."

"But it did wonders for growing the aerial legion of bareback wyvern fighters." All those World War II pilots received a pass if they agreed to serve in Hell's army.

"What are you going to do about the overload prob-lem? And have you thought about designating an heir?

You are not getting any younger." Even if the Devil didn't look a day over twenty-five. For a while, he'd sported the appearance of an older silver fox, but when the goody-two-shoes spell was peeled from him, so was the glamour hiding his true appearance.

Smoke curled from one nostril. "You aren't helping. I came to you to fix this."

"Can't. Sorry. Not sorry. And I'm going to make your day even shittier by letting you know that, topside, things are getting wonkier."

"In what way? I'm still trying to figure out how they got the caramel inside that chocolate bar."

No point in explaining machines to Dad again. His old-school upbringing didn't allow him to trust anything not made by hand. "Forget the caramel. Remember that thing you sent me on?"

"Did you find the strawberry-kiwi-flavored lube I like?"

"I told you they don't make it anymore. I am talking about the other thing. The zombie thing. Chris has no idea he's been raising the dead these last few weeks."

"He's lying."

"Is he?" she queried, giving her father a stare.

Lucifer stared off into space for a moment then frowned. "Hunh. I'll be damning myself; he isn't lying. The fucker has no idea."

"He also can't use his magic unless he's plastered."

"If he's only doing it while drunk, then tell him to sober up. He's screwing with my spell."

"I thought you took away his magic after the wedding to prevent him from being a threat." Chris didn't know. He just assumed his magic had gone away, and Bambi had told Isobel it was to hide him from his mother. Which was partially true.

Paranoid Lucifer worried about those two hooking up, which left him with two choices: kill the Antichrist before he came after his father, or remove the magic and make him as mundane as other humans.

"I did siphon the boy clean, which means what you're saying is impossible. He has no magic left."

"Says you. I'm telling you, he was raising the dead and lobbing the shit like he had a deep well. Is it possible it grew back?"

Lucifer frowned, creating a mighty unibrow only Gaia could love. "It shouldn't have returned this quickly."

"He is your blood. Could be he's got resistance to the spell. You might want to cast it again."

Lucifer's lips turned down. "I can't. He won't meet the conditions for a recast for seven years. I need the planets to be in a certain alignment."

"Then you might have a problem."

That drew his attention. "Has he said something about coming after me? I'll fucking kill him if he tries anything."

"My brother hasn't said dick. But I sense a great upheaval coming, and you know what the seers say."

"You mean *said*. Ursula is gone. Hell is safe. They

don't foresee me dealing with any major issues in the future."

"For now, but the horsemen ride, and we both know the seals on *her* prison broke." What they didn't know was where *she* escaped.

"*She* wouldn't dare act against me. Not after what happened last time."

"Or her resentment's been festering for all these years." At least a few centuries by Earth time, a blink really for the immortal, but given how time progressed differently in alternate dimensions, it could have been eons for her.

"I would know if she was out there in the world acting against me."

"Would you?"

"Of course, I would. Where does this doubt come from?"

"I met Famine last night. He might have fed on my confidence."

"Pesky fucker. Messing with my kids. Might be time to do something about him. Especially since you, of all my children, should never doubt me. Your father. I am the Lord of the Underworld, King of Sin. I know what's happening around me and on the mortal plane."

"Except you don't because you never suspected what Chris was doing."

"A mere blip," Lucifer stated.

"A blip?" Bambi turned to look at her father. "You had no clue. What else are you not seeing?"

"No more questioning me. I am the Dark Lord. The King of Lies. The—"

"Lucifer! Where's my pickles and poutine?" shouted an aggravated female voice.

"Coming, wench. Gotta go. Keep an eye on your brother."

As suddenly as her father had popped out of existence, Bambi just as quickly found herself back on Earth, speeding into a corner. She evaded a fiery death and then pondered the odd conversation with her dad, especially the fact that he couldn't see everything like he used to.

Was he losing his grip? Could a change in management be imminent? If that happened, which side would she be on?

10

Isobel sighed. "You can stop yelling. It won't help matters."

"Whose side are you on?" barked her grandfather.

"There are no sides," Isobel said, taking the spatula from him and rescuing the burning pancake. "The stove is not out to get you."

"Then why does it insist on burning things?"

"Since when do you try and cook?" she countered as she threw the pan into the sink and made him a bowl of cereal instead.

He took the spoon. "Our cook still hasn't returned. And I tire of this artificial..." *Crunch.* "Sugary." *Gulp. "Mmmm."*

Rasputin finally got something into his angry belly and mellowed out. The kitchen was safe until lunch, which would hopefully be easier, given she'd called a catering company to bring a platter of sandwiches.

It surprised her that Mother hadn't hired a new chef. As a matter of fact, she'd barely seen her mother of late. Even when she'd arrived in the middle of the night, her mother—who'd messaged her—didn't greet her; instead, she sent a note telling her to stay and keep an eye on Grandfather.

Only for a little while. Having moved out, Isobel wasn't ready at all to move back in. This wasn't her home anymore, especially since she had a house of her own—and a husband. The place didn't feel the same since she no longer saw the ghost of her father. Everything had changed the day she married.

The one thing that hadn't changed was the feeling of safety she got inside her childhood home. The layers of magic provided a soothing blanket of protection. She wouldn't have to worry about the horsemen appearing. Even Lucifer would hesitate before popping in.

Chris wouldn't be happy about it, though. At least it was only temporary.

As expected, Chris showed up first thing the next morning. Isobel left Goshen in the kitchen, munching on donuts, and skipped to the front door, only to encounter a thundercloud when she greeted her husband.

"There you are! What the fuck, duckie?"

"What's wrong?"

He gaped at her. "Wrong? You're here instead of at home. You left me!"

Her jaw dropped. "What are you talking about?"

Her expression creased in confusion. "Didn't you get my text?"

Judging by the look on his face, he hadn't.

"Do you even have your phone?" she asked.

"I, um, might have kind of forgotten it."

"It was beside your suitcase."

His expression cleared. "Aha! So you admit to packing it and tossing it out."

"Again, what are you talking about? I left your suitcase in the front hall with your phone. I would have brought it with me, but Charlie's sports car couldn't fit both pieces of luggage." At 4:00 a.m. there weren't many people a girl could call. Even Uber seemed a little dangerous given that the horsemen were out and about. Besides, Charlie owed her for running off and stranding her at that warehouse fight club.

"Fucking Jesus."

This time, she didn't correct it because it was becoming very clear that someone had an ulterior agenda. However, that didn't mean she wasn't going to toy with Chris. "I didn't fuck your cousin if that's what you're implying."

"You'd better not have," he snapped. "But I am still trying to understand why you left with him."

"I needed a ride, and he has a car."

"And why did you need a ride other than to leave me?"

"Again, I explained it in the text. On your phone.

Which you forgot," she added with a pointed look. "Mom called and asked me to watch Grandfather."

"You're kidding, right?"

"I wish, but no. My mom had to go away for a few days."

"Now."

"Yes, now."

"So you didn't leave me?" Judging by his expression, he really thought she had.

She laughed. "You silly man. Of course, I didn't leave you. As for your suitcase being outside, maybe Charlie thought it would fit in the car, and when it didn't, he left it on the porch."

"Or the dick wanted me to think something else." He glowered suspiciously.

"And you fell for it." She shook her head. "Really, Chris. You should know me better by now. Then again, maybe it's your guilt talking. After all, I'm not the one who's sneaking off at night."

"I'm not sneaking."

"Before you go down that lying road, let me add I followed you last night. When were you going to tell me what you were doing?"

The corners of his lips turned down. "I don't remember."

"Bull."

"It's the truth. I was drunk and blacked out."

Isobel blew a wet raspberry. "Please. I'm not that gullible. Don't forget, I know how much you can drink. You're like a fish when it comes to booze and drugs."

"Used to be. Now, I combine the two, and next thing I know, I'm waking up with a mouthful of dirt."

"I was so wasted I can't remember," she drawled sarcastically. "That seems like a pretty convenient excuse. Why not admit what you're doing? Admit you've been playing with your magic, which you've been swearing to me for months is gone."

"It is. Was." He stared at his hands. "I thought I couldn't touch it at all. But Bambi said—"

"What's your sister got to do with this?"

"She showed me a video. Of me. Last night."

"And?"

He shrugged, his wide shoulders lifting and falling with defeat. "I was doing some badass shit with dead people and magic. But even seeing it, I don't remember."

For a moment, she stared at him, noting his drooping shoulders, his tight lips. "I'll be damned, you're telling the truth, aren't you?"

"Sadly enough."

She sighed, especially since she knew that even if he weren't, his woes were of Lucifer's making. Telling him would serve no purpose. He already despised his dad. "Come with me. Let's get you in a shower."

"*Woof.*" Goshen barked. The big furball had finished his breakfast and stood behind her, his muzzle ringed with icing sugar.

Isobel cast her dog a glance and shook a finger. "No, you can't join us. You know what happened last time." The giant furball had attacked the detachable showerhead, chomping on it and causing it to sever and spray all over until she could finally shut it off.

The largest set of puppy eyes regarded her. Testing her resistance.

She melted. "If you're a good puppy, I'll put the sprinkler on later."

"*Woof.*"

The dog bounded off, probably to spend some time with his girlfriend, her mom's Yorkie, Queenie—who had mellowed out since getting with the hellhound.

Before she and Chris could make it to their room, her mother waylaid them. A woman in her late fifties yet appearing more like her early thirties, Marya's blonde hair held hints of platinum rather than gray, her features were still mostly smooth, and her figure, dressed properly in a blouse and pressed slacks, was trim. What stuck out, though, was the fact that her mother had missed a button. That never happened, and since when did her mom go around with flushed cheeks?

"I thought you were already gone," Isobel said.

"Shortly. I see you brought *him* to join you." Mother had treated Chris with icy indifference since he insisted they move out of the mansion and live on their own.

Being a shit disturber, Chris offered her his most

charming smile. "If it isn't my favorite mother-in-law. You're looking less haggard than usual, Marya. Did you bathe in a vat of anti-aging cream?"

"Blood of virgins, actually," Mother replied, utterly deadpan.

"Surprised you managed to find any in this day and age," he muttered.

"Did you want something, Mother?" Isobel asked. "I wouldn't want you to be late for your trip."

"I was just about to leave but wanted to advise you we'll be having guests for dinner on Friday."

"Who cares? We'll be back home by then," Chris remarked.

Whereas Isobel, spotting the sly gleam in her mother's eyes, asked, "Who?"

"Just a few friends. People you both might like to meet."

"How many is a few?" asked Isobel while pondering the fact that Mother had used the word "both." What was she planning?

"Nothing big. Under fifty."

Which Mother truly did consider a small gathering.

"We'll be there," she announced.

"Excellent." Mother beamed before sailing off with a swish of her perfectly pressed slacks.

Chris whispered, "Tell me you just lied."

"We are going," she said, heading in the direction of her room once again.

"You know I hate your mother's stuffy parties."

"We all do, but as the Antichrist, it's important you make an appearance. How else are you going to gain allies?"

"I'm confused. I thought you didn't want me ruling the world. But lately, you've been sending mixed signals."

"I don't want you killing everyone. Never said you shouldn't rule. Even if you don't go to war, it never hurts to have connections. Some of Mother's guests own islands in tropical places."

"So we're playing nice for a free vacation."

"No, we're playing nice because if you're having blackouts, and things seem too quiet, then it probably means we're about to have fun."

"Fun?" A hopeful glint entered his gaze. "Think I'll get to use that new sword I ordered?"

"I do. Which means, I'd better hurry up and finish that cape I've been making for you." Something to rival Lucifer's own.

"No cape." Chris shook his head. "They are the number one cause of injury among superheroes."

"But you're not a hero." She peeked at him and winked. "You're the villain."

11

A VILLAIN?

If ever there were a word to make an Antichrist stand tall, his wife had used it. Still, shouldn't a villain remember his bad deeds?

The thought plagued Chris, especially since he had to wonder if his blackouts were because of his mommy meddling again. Something kept nagging at him—out of sight, out of mind. It tickled the edges of his consciousness, but he couldn't grab hold of it and drag it into the light.

Rather than fret about it, because worry was for losers, he chased his wife up the stairs.

She still had a room in her old family home. And by room, he meant suite, with a sitting area and a massive bathroom made for debauchery.

She already had the water going and her clothes on

the floor by the time he reached her. His outfit joined hers in a dirty pile seconds after.

However, when he went to grab hold of her and draw her close, her nose wrinkled.

"Soap first. You smell like a zombie." Which to the uninformed wasn't the most attractive aroma.

For those out there who groaned because she made him wait, that waiting included her hands, covered in soap, lathering his body. They skimmed over his frame, familiar with his shape; yet each time she touched him, it was as if she discovered him anew, her exploration thorough, tantalizing. As if they were indulging their first time. Each caress drew a gasp or a moan or a shiver. The press of her lips on his skin branded him as hers.

When she dropped to her knees to worship his erect cock, he threw back his head and enjoyed it. She knew how to please him, her hand gripping the base of his shaft, a tight fist to hold him while her mouth did decadent things to him.

She ate his cock as if he were a delectable treat. Licking the fat head of it. Running her tongue up and down the length. Her hand kneading his balls when she took him deep into her mouth.

She sucked hard and kept a rhythm going, bobbing her head every so often, letting the flat edge of her teeth graze the flesh.

When his balls tightened, and his body went rigid, she didn't stop. She sucked him harder, if that were possible; as if determined to suck every last drop.

And then it was her turn. Because this was one thing in his life that Chris was never selfish about. Sharing was caring. And eating her was divine.

The bench in the shower, which she liked to use to shave her legs, was at just the right height for her to sit and spread her thighs. He knelt before her and buried his face against her mound. Spread her pink nether lips with his tongue and gave her the tongue-lashing she so rightly deserved.

She pulled his hair.

Squirmed.

Cried out more than once.

And when she came against his tongue, yelling his name, it was as if he came again, a ghostly orgasm on a different level than the physical, but just as satisfying.

While the shower she'd insisted on did much to revive him, and the oral was stupendous, even after a nap, his arms wrapped around his wife's naked body, he couldn't help but mull over what she'd said.

Am I really such a villain? Thus far, he'd not done anything truly evil by the standard of evil deeds—which apparently was a huge tome kept in Hell that listed every possible sin. Only rarely was something new added to its venerated pages.

Or so he'd heard. His father had yet to invite him to read it for himself. Asshole.

He certainly didn't feel like a villain most days.

Villains didn't have to do the dishes when their wives went out for ladies' night. Nor did they pick up giant dog poop from a canine that purposely digested his food in the most obscene way possible. Even the thickest of masks didn't hide the stench.

None of that was evil.

What of his nocturnal visits to the underground, supernatural fight club? Did those count if he couldn't remember them?

Surely, villains never suffered from doubt like he did.

More worrisome was the fact that the more he learned, the less he knew. When younger, his future seemed simple. Being the Antichrist equaled taking over the world. The reality, though, proved more complicated.

Was it his destiny? Or had he lost that chance months ago in that crypt when he made that promise to her father?

Isobel doesn't care if I want to rule the world. She'd more or less given him permission, which was totally cool. Now if only he knew how to go about doing that.

"You need an army."

The whisper could have been his own.

"It is time to gather the forces, for there is a battle on the horizon. A grand reckoning is coming. All my enemies shall be destroyed."

Now that definitely wasn't his thought. He rolled out of bed and into the bathroom, easing the door shut behind him before whispering out loud, "Mother, is that you?" He felt like such a moron. Talking to thin air. Imagining voices in his head. But he knew all too well that sometimes those voices were real.

"Mother?"

For a moment, there was no reply, and then a chilled wind filled the bathroom despite the sealed window. It pimpled his skin and shriveled his dick.

A glance at the mirror showed it fogging over, and his breath emerged in a white mist. Either someone had cranked the AC, or shit was happening. He could have shouted with glee. Instead, he adopted a stoic mien.

When the voice came, it surrounded him, a cold hug that made his balls turtle, tucked so tightly, they might never drop again.

"Did you think I'd forgotten you, my son?"

Shit, it was the psycho herself. "Long time, no talk, Mother."

"Is it? Seems like only yesterday."

Ominous words. "Where are you?" *Please say prison, because I am not ready to deal with you.*

"Right here, my son."

A scream almost escaped him as the fog in the mirror suddenly cleared, and a woman appeared. A familiar woman.

"Have we met?" *Met and he'd not realized?*

The eyes, black as night—cold, too—perused him. "Is it time for you to remember?"

Remember what? What had she done to him now? "Why must you always talk in circles? Would it fucking kill you to give me a straight answer?"

"I can't die."

A disturbing reply that still didn't tell him anything. "Why are you here?"

"You called me."

"Is that all it takes?"

"Now that the magical cloak hiding you has thinned, you have only to think of me and I will come to you, *my son*."

Chilling, especially since she paired it with a creepy freaking smile. He retained his masculinity, barely, and touched the mirrored reflection. He half expected his hand to go through, but glass met his fingers. "How are you doing that?" Because it was a pretty cool trick. He could totally have fun with it at Halloween. Imagine someone saying, "bloody Mary" and getting him instead.

"Come to me, my son, and I'll teach you."

"Yeah, I don't think so. I've seen what you like to do with bodies." Especially dead ones.

"I have no need of your fleshy container anymore."

"What's that supposed to mean?"

"I walk the world in my own body. The seals that held me prisoner are broken. I am free again."

"Impossible." He'd kept the last seal intact even if it meant lying to Isobel about her father. Her daddy's soul was the only thing holding his mother's prison closed. The only thing protecting the world.

"Someone had the courage to do what you could not." Disdain curled her lip.

"Who?"

"Someone who isn't afraid of your destiny."

Cryptic words to ponder later. "What happened to Isobel's father?" Had his soul gone to a better place?

"I don't know, and I don't care."

Not exactly surprising. "What's your plan now that you've been sprung?"

"I plan to have my revenge."

"Against who?"

"Your father, for one. And all those who helped imprison me."

"You can't kill the Devil."

"Who said anything about killing? There are other paths to revenge. You have much to learn."

"And you're going to teach me?" He didn't let her disapproval hurt—much. As if he cared what a crazy demi-goddess thought.

"We don't have time for lessons. The horsemen ride even as we speak, sowing discord, readying the way."

"Did it ever occur to you that maybe, just maybe, you should play it cool for a while? You know, enjoy life, not try and destroy the world. Maybe relax a bit on a beach, sipping piña coladas?"

"I have already spent too much time waiting," Mother snapped.

"You do realize you're setting yourself up for more jail time if you continue on this path. Do you want to be locked away for decades again?" Since he didn't recollect her, he could only assume that she'd been incarcerated while he was still young. Clarice, the woman he'd believed was his mother for years, had never spoken of her.

"You think it was mere decades?" Laughter, discordant and sharp, erupted. His mother's face creased in mirth, her eyes black and cold. "Time passes differently in some planes. I spent eons in that abyss. Expended all my strength birthing you and pushing you forth out of that prison. Then eons more waiting for my son to come into his power. For him to rescue his mother."

"If you're just here to blame me because I didn't break you out of prison, then you can go away right now. I don't need your shit. I've got enough on my plate to deal with."

A sneer pulled at her lips. "Ah, yes, such a busy schedule, digging holes. Which seems like a waste of energy given you're going to need those bodies to fight."

"Fight who? You?"

More tinkling laughter. "You can't hope to win against me. The more time I spend in this dimension, the stronger I get. Soon, I'll have my revenge, and you'll have to make a choice."

She didn't need to say it for him to know what choice she meant.

In, or out.

Did he side with his mother and go after his father? Or the other way around? He kind of hated them both at the moment, although—if he had to give the edge to one parent over the other—at least his mom had given him up in hopes that he'd have a better life than eternal damnation.

"Where are you now?" he asked.

"Close. I'll see you soon, my son." With that chilling remark, the mirror shimmered and once again showed his reflection. Scruffy hair standing on end, his nipples hard enough to cut glass. Next time he saw her, he'd better wear a parka.

Next time...

Was she really nearby?

If Mother had told the truth and she escaped, then that meant Isobel's father no longer held the prison door shut. The man had sacrificed his life, using his own essence to keep it sealed. If that seal were broken, did that mean he'd died, and his soul moved on?

Only one way to find out. Leaving Isobel asleep, Chris dressed and then headed to the crypt.

He'd not been there since that night when he and Isobel went looking for her missing father. The night she didn't remember because her grandfather altered her memories.

Two of them bound by oath, the lie a burning acid reflux that surely wasn't a guilty conscience.

But Chris remembered, and the fact that he'd lied to her about it gave him heartburn.

He didn't go alone. Goshen, that big hairy mutt, followed by his side, and while he'd never say it aloud, he was glad for the big fucker's company. The last time he'd been to the crypt, he'd encountered some of his mother's minions. The horsemen had done their best to make him fail in his mission.

This time, no doubt crept into his thoughts, urging him to turn back. Nor did the foliage show anything but the signs of fall approaching.

Twilight fell early this time of year, which meant he walked in near darkness, and yet he could see enough to find his way to the crypt hidden in the forest on Rasputin land. A tomb that didn't try to lead him astray, unlike the previous attempt.

The magic that had once kept it hidden from prying eyes no longer pushed against his skin. The door yielded easily to his touch, the dust within coated the floor, showing no signs of disruption. The once lit torches were dead. He used the lighter he kept in his pocket to light one, the sputtering flame fighting against the thick gloom.

In the room below the crypt, he noted that the altar that had once held Isobel's father's body loomed bare.

The magic in this place, the last seal holding the prison, was gone.

His mother was free.

And what did he do? Did he scream, "Run for your lives"? Did he blubber on the floor, a terrified mess?

Nope. He whistled as he strode back to the mansion. Hands in his pockets. Nonchalant as you please.

Looked as if he might need that cape his wife was making, after all.

THE DOORBELL RANG, and while Goshen perked his head, he didn't remove himself from her lap. Given he weighed a ton, Isobel wasn't going anywhere.

Before she could holler for Chris, he ran past the doorway to the living room shouting, "I got it."

Did he expect someone? It would be a first. Her husband didn't go out of his way to be social and invite people over. Ever.

Therefore, she assumed she was dreaming when he reappeared a moment later with Charlie.

Goshen bared his teeth and growled.

"Um, what's he doing here?" she asked. Because the last time those two had gotten together, it had ended with Chris trying to rearrange Charlie's face, and later with fireballs trying to singe his ass.

Chris, looking remarkably relaxed, replied, "I asked him to come over."

Definitely hallucinating. But she went along with it. "What for?"

"Mother's loose. I thought perhaps between the pair of us, we could find and stop her before she really gets started on fucking up the world."

"Did you drug me?" she asked. "Because that made no sense."

"On the contrary," Charlie interjected, making himself at home by flinging himself onto the couch across from her. This finally dislodged Goshen, who parked himself in front of her, staring at the Son of God. "He's showing initiative."

Her husband, showing initiative? Something was definitely not right.

Chris chose a spot beside her, his arm casually draped over her shoulders, marking her as his possession. The feminist in her sniffed in annoyance. The woman in her purred.

"Whatever my mom has planned, we have to stop it," Chris stated.

What was with this *we* shtick? "How?" she asked. "Because unless something has changed in the last twenty-four hours, you still don't have a handle on your magic."

"But, apparently, it's there if I need it."

"You mean if you get wasted. And who's to say you'll want to work against your mother when that happens? Maybe you'll join her, and you'll both want to end the world."

"That's where Jesus comes in." Chris jabbed his finger at Charlie. "He's going to make sure I don't turn into a psychotic despot."

Her gaze bounced between the men, even more lost than before. "By doing what?"

"I don't know. But I figured if I was going to call anyone, then an arms dealer was a good start."

"He sells weapons; he doesn't use them. Charlie is horrible at fighting."

"True." Charlie didn't even deny it. "But on top of my weapons, I do have access to the archangels and Heaven's army."

Her brow creased. "Please don't tell me you've asked Charlie to kill you if you turn evil."

"Not kill!" Charlie exclaimed. "I do have morals."

"Nasty things, those morals, but in this case, they work to my advantage. The plan is he'll detain me if I go evil. Put me in rehab until I regain my senses."

Isobel shoved away from Chris. "This is the most moronic plan I've heard." And she wanted nothing to do with it. She strode out of the room, angry and afraid.

What was Chris thinking? While Charlie might not bear him ill will, the archangels wouldn't be as lenient. Elyon's army wasn't known for second chances. The number of fallen angels attested to that fact.

When unleashed, they had one purpose: destroy evil. If they thought Chris was a problem, they wouldn't hesitate to kill him, no matter what Charlie ordered. Which scared her. *I don't want to lose him.*

So what's my brilliant plan? Because Chris did have a point. If his mother were loose, then that wouldn't bode well for the world. Or him.

With her mind in turmoil, she went looking for the one person who would see straight to the heart of the matter and tell her what to do. Grandfather didn't bother himself with the concept of good or evil, but the fact of whether it benefited the family or not. And by benefit, he'd want the solution that kept Isobel and the other Rasputins alive—and powerful.

Isobel found Grandfather in his lab, puttering around, playing with smoking vials, the liquid in them glowing. He dropped in pinches of this and that— powdered tongue of an imp, the eyeball of a gorgon, a sliver from a unicorn's hoof. As a child, she used to read with wide eyes the fascinating labels in his locked apothecary, a huge wooden armoire with drawers and shelves filled with fantastical ingredients. Many of the items were bought on the cryptid black market. Others, he and Mother had collected themselves. Given the gruesome nature of a few, Isobel preferred not to know what the process involved.

"He's insane!" she declared, walking in.

The old man, his bald pate gleaming as he leaned over to blow on a steaming bowl, didn't immediately reply.

"I said he's insane."

"Who?" Absently asked as he dropped a single red drop into the concoction.

"My husband, of course."

"And?" he asked, lifting his head, the monocle rendering his eye huge.

"And I don't want an insane husband."

"Why not? What do you have against the insane?" Grandfather asked. "You do realize, of the family, you're the only one who hasn't received a diagnosis that you're slightly off-kilter. Although they might revise your last prognosis given your marriage." Because, apparently, no sane woman would marry the Devil's son.

"Did you know Chris is, right now, concocting a stupid plan to find his mother?"

"What's so stupid about finding her? She did, after all, birth him. Why wouldn't he want to reconnect with his roots?"

"Because she's evil. She wants to destroy the world."

"Not destroy. She wants revenge. If the world is destroyed in the process..." Rasputin shrugged.

"Seriously? That's all you have to say about it?"

"What did you expect?" Grandfather asked, fixing her with a stare. "You cannot expect her to forget her vendetta merely because you ask her to."

"Then what am I supposed to do?"

"Stay on her good side by keeping her only son happy."

She already planned to. "But what of the fate of the world?"

"What of it? The world—actually anyone outside this house and this family—isn't your problem." He bent back to the bowl and dropped something else into it before running his hand over the top, mumbling.

"Aren't you the slightest bit worried?" she asked. "If evil succeeds in winning—"

"Then we'll join it. Really, Isobel. Have you not paid attention to our family history at all? We are not heroes, Granddaughter. Nor are we kind, benevolent, or particularly caring unless it concerns one of our own. We choose the side of whomever we think will prevail. We do whatever we must to ensure we survive. And, really, I don't understand this caterwauling. You were the one who chose to marry the Son of Perdition. What did you expect?"

She expected...to be his queen, but had never really thought of how she'd get there. "I didn't expect him to die fighting against his mother." Or, worse, be possessed by her.

"Why the assumption she'll kill him? He's her only son. Did it never occur to either of you that perhaps she only wants to help him achieve his goals?"

"You said it yourself; she wants revenge."

"And she very well might get it. If she does, let's

say she manages to eliminate Lucifer. Then that leaves his son to take his place. With you as his queen."

"I don't want to become queen like that." She didn't particularly care for the Devil; however, she couldn't condone the killing of her father-in-law.

"In that case, why marry a man destined to rule the world and Hell? You had to realize there would be violence involved."

It shamed her to realize she'd not really thought further than the fact that she supported Chris. "Let's say his mother does achieve her vengeance. We don't know what will happen next. What if her plans don't include Christopher?" Or Isobel.

"Have you asked her?"

"Ask her how? We don't even know where she is," she yelled, fists clenched, her ire burning hot. The bowl in front of Grandfather shattered.

"Enough of your childish tantrum," Grandfather boomed. "You made your choice when you married him. Now hold your chin high, accept your role, and cease the whining."

Whining? He considered her worrying about the fate of everyone whining? Her anger grew, and the room trembled. Glass broke as furniture wobbled, tilting things onto the floor. Items broke as wood and plaster shifted.

Rasputin lost his smile and scowled. "That's better. Get angry. Use it. You'll need that in the coming days."

That quickly, her ire vanished. "Why? What did you see?"

Grandfather didn't speak, and yet, suddenly, she saw. Saw Chris sitting on a throne, a seat made of skulls and fire. As for Isobel, she stood by his side wearing a crown.

In Hell.

13

CHRIS AND JESUS didn't accomplish much during their pow-wow other than demolishing a case of beer. Apparently, having been raised on wine, the guy could hold his liquor. Whereas, Chris, who used to be able to drink anyone under the table and still recite the alphabet backwards, lost time after an easy half-dozen brews.

Tonight, he didn't limit himself on the bottles he chugged. Knew what might happen if he tipped off the edge. Kind of hoped it would happen.

Sure, drinking when he had important shit to figure out—like finding his mommy and deciphering her plans—might be stupid, but some of his best ideas came while drunk. His problem was recalling all the details the following day because he never wrote them down. Or when he did, the lipstick on a napkin proved fairly unreadable. Who knew how many millions of dollars he'd lost out on because he couldn't remember the brilliant math accomplished the night before.

In his world, drinking and brainstorming went hand in hand—if he had the right person to bounce ideas with. Turned out his cousin, despite his heavenly connections, didn't have many original ideas. You'd think a guy whose company developed grenades camouflaged to look mundane—like a cell phone or a lipstick—would have all kinds of associations. A spy network at the very least. *I mean, come on, the guy has access to angels.*

Whom Jesus couldn't order around because his dad, as his cousin had said, "Is a tightwad who won't relinquish any power to me because he says I make the wrong kinds of friends." Jesus stared at Chris with eyes that blazed blue. "It was two thousand years ago! I was just a kid in the grand scheme of immortality. But am I allowed to forget the fact I trusted Judas and he screwed me over?" His cousin slashed a hand. "Nope. There're books detailing my mistakes. Movies showing me hanging on that cross. Everywhere I turn, it's shoved in my face."

Chris stared at him. "Dude, that sucks." At least the prophecies about the Antichrist had him doing cool shit.

What if I fail? Would there be a movie about him, too? Or would he only rate a made-for-television special? And most importantly, what actor would they cast for his part?

Apart from hashing out who would play them best in autobiographies—and Jesus lamenting the lack of hot and easy chicks in Heaven—they did discuss Chris's mom a bit.

Very little.

"No idea where she is," Jesus said.

"Can you at least give me a name?" asked Chris because, somehow, calling her psycho seemed a tad like poking the bear.

"Haven't the slightest. Dad won't say."

Why the big secret?

There existed another person he could ask. Lucifer would know. But that meant reaching out first. Caving first in the game of I-can-go-longest-without-calling.

Fuck that. Chris would win the competition for most stubborn.

Which meant that he and Jesus, being at an impasse and unable to make plans, had only one thing they could actually do.

Drink.

Given how many beers they'd put away, Chris kind of expected to black out and wake up covered in grave dirt. Instead, he woke in bed beside his wife. A nice place to be with naked limbs, soft titties, and an erection poking against her backside that she wasn't shying away from.

A good sign because it meant that, despite their small spat the previous day, she'd chosen not to remain pissed.

Someone just might get morning sex. His favorite kind, right along with shower sex, car sex, public-place sex, and his most favorite: with-his-wife-anywhere sex.

"Hi," he said, using his slickest voice.

She rolled over in bed and faced him, tousled hair framing her face. "Hi right back at you, stud muffin." She winked. "How's the King of Fierce Countenance today?"

"Uh, fine." If confused. Since when did his duckie use corny lines on him?

"I wondered how you'd feel given you tied a good one on last night."

So many beers. So many staggers to the bathroom to pee. But was that the only thing he did? "Did I go wandering again?" Because he'd asked Jesus to follow and record him if he did. But the guy had been pretty wasted, too. Chris had better check his social media and see what the Son of God posted. He vaguely recalled something about a full moon and not the kind in the sky.

"No wandering," Isobel said, reaching out to brush the hair off his forehead. "Not this time. I found you passed out in the bathroom using the toilet as a pillow."

"How did I get to bed?"

"I have my ways." She smiled as she rolled atop him.

"How come you're not angry?" he asked.

"I talked to my grandfather. He calmed me down."

"Rasputin calmed you?" A frown pulled at his face.

"We are talking about the skinny, bald, angry guy, right?"

"Grandfather isn't always angry."

Chris arched a single brow.

Her lips quirked. "It's just how he is. But if you listen, you'll realize it's less anger and more common sense in the face of stupidity."

"He told you I was stupid?"

Laughter spilled from his duckie. "No. He told me I was being stupid. He reminded me of who I am and the fact that I always knew who you were and yet chose to be with you."

"I did kind of say I wouldn't chase my destiny anymore, though."

"Even though you're not chasing, destiny is coming for you. I can't change that." Isobel shrugged. "Therefore, I need to embrace it. To support you in any way I can."

This sudden understanding brought a frown. "Who are you, and what did you do with my wife?" Seriously. Was Isobel possessed?

"Joke all you want. I mean it. I'm going to help you, and help you find your mother."

"Maybe she's best left hidden," he mused aloud. They could leave each other alone. She could have her half of the world; he'd just keep his tiny pocket. They never had to meet.

"Hiding means we could possibly be surprised. No. We have to be more proactive."

"And exactly how do you propose to find my mother?" he asked, placing his hands on her hips. Her very naked hips. Why were they wasting time talking when they could be fucking?

"By getting you to use magic again, for one."

He frowned. "But I can't."

"That's a lie. We both know you can."

"When drunk. I'm not drunk now."

"Maybe it's not the booze that frees it but the fact you're relaxed and letting loose. What if..." She ground her hips against him and let her thighs fall to either side of his body, pressing her damp core against his cock. "We try another way of accessing it."

"You wanna have sex to see if I can touch my magic?" The idea totally worked for him.

"Yes. I want you to let go. Relax. Ease your mind."

Instead, he tensed. "What if I relax too much, and she gets inside my head?"

Isobel crouched over him, a taunt on her lips. "Who's the man?"

"I'm the man."

"Who's the baddest?"

He smiled. "I'm the baddest."

"Who's going to make me scream his name?"

Fuck me. She was going to yell it so loudly, the windows would rattle.

He wasted no time, spinning her onto her back, his lips blazing a trail down her belly, the skin soft and yet, under it, a solid ridge of muscle. His woman kept fit. So sexy.

He loved watching her doing her yoga, her body bent in beautiful ways. Loved seeing her spar inside the home gym she'd created, her body twisting and turning, the sweat glistening on her body.

My body. It was his, every inch of it, and he claimed it with his lips. Pressing them against her flesh, branding her. Her legs parted for his body as he nestled between her thighs.

He rubbed the fur of his beard against that inner skin, loving how her back arched, her breath sucked in with an audible gasp, and her fingers clutched at the sheets.

He blew on her, the hotness of his breath causing a chain reaction of squirming and moaning, but the best part was the moisture glistening on her pink nether lips.

My lips.

He blew again, hot, steamy air followed by a long, wet lick. Some people called it honey. He called it ambrosia, the thing only gods drank. He was a god, and this ambrosia belonged to him.

He lapped at her, spreading the pink shells, delving into the channel that loved to squeeze around his dick. He throbbed.

Oh, how he fucking throbbed.

But this was about her. His woman. Her pleasure.

This wasn't his relaxation, not when he tried to

hold on when her lips nibbled at him. Not when he held back, every muscle in him straining until she creamed his cock. He only truly felt at ease when eating his gorgeous wife's cunt.

His tongue flicked at her nubbin of pleasure. She jumped.

He licked it again and again. Held her down when she would have bucked.

He worked that button of hers, sucking and pinching it with his lips. He knew what she liked, and he gave it to her, penetrating her with two fingers, groaning against her flesh as her channel gripped tightly.

It would feel so good on his cock. But he wanted her to come on his tongue. Wanted to feel it.

He lapped faster and faster. She gasped. She clawed at the sheets. She began panting his name.

And then she came. A hard clamp on his fingers, then undulating waves of pleasure as she keened, her orgasm making her loud.

When she began to slow down, he nipped at her clit, put his heavy arms across her lower belly, and worked that sensitive spot.

Her sex stopped quivering and tightened.

She mewled. "Now. Fuck me. Now!"

He slid up her body and rammed in his hard cock, gave it to her a little rough because that was how she liked it after oral.

She grabbed his shoulders and dug in her fingers. "Fuck me."

She also got dirty.

He thrust into her, hard strokes, deep strokes, the kind that rammed against her G-spot. That had her gasping for air.

Had him grunting to hold on. And then she squeezed him, fisted his cock tightly as she came again.

Only then did he follow. His body tensed, one final deep thrust, and then he soared. He dropped out of his body and was a warm cloud above it. Isobel's hot cumulus merged with his, and he heard her whispering, "Call the magic. Let it burn through you. Burn through us both."

He didn't even think, just pulled, yanked all the power he could feel around him, let it fill him up.

It still filled him as he dropped back into his body. He tingled and had a hard time holding on to it.

"It's slipping," he murmured.

"Let's see if we can't stop that." She clamped her legs around his hips while her arms wrapped his neck and...she made him expand.

Not his flesh, but his magic. It was as if she pushed even more into him. Built up the reservoir he could draw, and he opened his mouth at the pleasure-pain of it.

"It's too much."

"Just a bit more."

"Too much, I can't hold it."

"You can. We did it before," she insisted and shoved more into him until he burned.

He yelled without a sound. He exploded but stayed intact.

The power burned through him, burned away all pretense, all the dark corners. Even the bespelled ones.

Everything burned away, all the cobwebs hiding his secrets.

He remembered it all. His mother. The fighting. Even attacking his wife.

"How is it you manage to always forgive me?" he said.

In that moment of closeness, she didn't have to ask what he meant. "I love you."

A simple reply. The only one.

"I would do anything for you." The fierce words spat from him.

"I know. And speaking of doing, we have to get ready."

"Ready for what?" he asked, glancing at the clock. Two o'clock, and he'd guess it was the afternoon given the light streaming through the cracks in the curtains.

"Ready for the party, silly. Remember, Mother told us about it."

Already Friday? He groaned. "Do I have to?"

"Yes. But don't worry, I'll make it worth your while."

More like made him forget with more hot sex. Her oral talents in the shower didn't just blow his mind.

The drying off after also proved tons of fun—to the point he *almost* forgot.

It was Isobel who reminded him to get ready as she poured herself out of bed, naked limbs stretching, the smile she bestowed on him the kind only shared between lovers.

"Where are you going?" Because, despite all the action, he could go for another round.

"Mother's plane is running late, so I promised I'd keep an eye on the preparations and staff."

"I have a staff that could use your attention, too." Because when it came to Isobel, he never got enough.

"Maybe later," she replied with a wink. He watched as she dressed and left the room. He moved almost immediately after.

It's time. He'd been fucking with Isobel when he pretended he'd forgotten about the party. He remembered. Remembered everything.

Something had happened during sex when he accessed his magic. Isobel had acted as an amplifier. And, somehow, the intensity of the magic destroyed all the spells on him. More than one, he might add.

Spells to hide him. Spells to make him forget —forget the dark chasm where he'd been born. The soft whispers of his mother as she kissed him once before sending him away. The screaming pain as he was torn with great sacrifice from the blood of his followers in his mother's prison. Then hidden. Hidden from everyone so that he might grow to manhood. Spelled to keep his magic subdued.

All manner of magical manipulation to get him to reach this point in his destiny.

All gone now. *I am now 100 percent me.* And then some.

Chris also had abilities he'd not had before, skills that he'd once had a hard time accessing. Not anymore.

Magic coursed through his veins. Power tickled his fingertips. It took but a thought to make it take shape.

He lifted his hand and looked at it. A ball of dancing fire sat on his palm. Concentrating on it changed its color. He could also expand its size.

That might come in handy, and just in time, too. He had a feeling he might need magic soon. Anticipation imbuing the very air around him spoke of important things about to happen.

For once, he would be ready.

An hour later, when Isobel returned to the room, her eyes widened upon seeing him. "Don't you look dashing," she remarked, taking in his suit. "But the party isn't for another two hours."

"I'm running early." A jab at his father, who took signs of promptness as a personal insult.

"Where did you get the threads?" she asked, stripping from her casual wear, her lithe frame hidden at moments by the golden cascade of her hair. She'd chosen to let it grow, and with a little magical help, it now hit the top of her buttocks. As if sensing the direction of his stare, she bent over, the perfect globes just asking for a bite.

"Your mother had one of the staff bring it. Said it belonged to your father when he was younger."

Which was kind of morbid, but something like a well-made suit never went out of style. At least according to Marya. He'd grumbled when his mother-in-law had left orders for a tailor to waylay him and insisted on having it sized for him.

His excuse of, "I'm sure I've got something kind of clean kicking around I can wear," not quite cutting it.

He'd put up a valiant verbal fight but, in the end, had allowed himself to be dressed in an Armani suit.

Looked damned good, too. And it was about time because here was the thing: people had a point when they claimed that to be a leader, you should look like one.

Folks wouldn't want to follow a simple guy in threadbare jeans and rude-gesture T-shirts. How could he expect people to give him armies if he didn't look the part?

"Looking for an army now?" Isobel noted.

He blinked. "Did I say that out loud?"

"Yes, along with some look-like-a-leader thing. Which, by the way, you do. Look. Leaderish that is. Does that mean you know who my mother has invited to this soiree?"

"Nope, but given she's got an army of staff marching around snapping salutes, I'd say they are important." Which piqued his interest. Especially once he saw the cases of wine being unpacked.

"Well, whatever the reason for the suit, you look delicious. As in, find-me-later delectable. I won't wear panties." Wink.

Talk about an instant boner. "I am available now."

"But I'm not," she said with a laugh as she danced out of his reach. "Time to make myself presentable."

More like make herself look dangerous. His surely weren't the only eyeballs that practically fell out of his head when Isobel deigned to descend the stairs as the first of the guests arrived.

Chris had always known she was beautiful. Elegant. Perfect.

But the woman descending the steps...she was temptation itself. She wore a black dress, form-fitting, hugging her every curve, the front a loose swatch of fabric that hung in a cowl that showcased the edges of her breasts. The material skimmed over her hips and fell in a slim sheath, but when she walked, the thigh-high slit showed off her trim leg.

Damn.

Someone throw a blanket on her because he didn't want to share.

The good news? *I don't have to.* Because she was his wife. He took pride in the fact that people coveted her. Let them gaze upon what they couldn't have. Let them envy him.

Chris met her at the bottom of the stairs and held

out his hand. When she slid hers into his, a shiver went through him, the kind he always enjoyed every time they touched. A missing link now making a return since it had disappeared after the wedding.

Interesting.

Also of interest, the way everyone watched and whispered. He held in a smile as he heard the words "regal," "nothing like his father," "...hear we're having raspberry mousse for dessert." Mmm. His favorite.

They spent only a short moment nodding their heads at people, offering quiet smiles before heading into the dining area, the names of those he met a jumble in his head.

The dining room chosen for the event wasn't the intimate one. They were in a massive space, lavishly decorated in pink and gold paper that screamed "old money." The fifty-person table made of stone, massive. The army to serve them the five courses, plentiful.

The wine, so delicious. And he needed that libation when he saw the layers of cutlery. Why couldn't they just put out one fork, one knife, and one spoon?

Isobel leaned close and murmured, "Start on the outside, work your way in."

"Even though I'm left-handed?"

"Just do what I do."

Who would have thought he'd wish someone had taught him table etiquette? Then again, he'd never imagined sitting down at such a fancy dinner with people dressed in tuxedos and expensive gowns. The jewelry alone probably totaled millions. Maybe even billions.

It might have made a lesser man feel inadequate. Good thing Chris knew he was more important than all of them.

The first pledge to join his legion—which almost caused him to choke on the fine wine—came before the first course and by an elderly gent seated across from Chris. Some royal or whatnot from Europe.

The old fellow, his sparse hair combed over a bald spot, leaned forward, his expression earnest. "Promise me a spot in the inner ring when you ascend to power."

As a person who liked to announce shocking things to people for shits and giggles, Chris took this offer with aplomb. "The inner ring is for my most devoted. Why should I give it to you? How many legions do you offer to the cause?"

"My country will loan all its troops for a spot in the first ring."

"Which is how many exactly?"

A sizeable number was mentioned, and Chris did his best not to blink, especially since this was his first offer of support. Never mind that he still didn't know what he'd do with them. "It's adequate. I suppose."

But the elderly royal wasn't done. "I also have a daughter—"

Isobel leaned into him, her body tense, her voice quite icy. "Perhaps you didn't read the announcement in the paper." A two-page spread in most major news outlets worldwide. "He's married. To me."

"Really? I hadn't heard."

Lie. But Chris didn't mention it because he would wager that Isobel already knew.

"You don't want me as your enemy," his wife replied icily.

The cold words warmed his blood. What a truly formidable woman he'd married, and to think, he'd met her by chance in a cemetery. Together, they were almost invincible.

"Awfully sorry for the mistake." The old guy backpedaled.

His wife responded with a pert, "My husband will mull over your offer. We wouldn't want to be hasty."

Hasty about what? Chris finally had someone who wanted to help him. He just didn't know why. Why would that guy pledge his aid out of the blue?

He tried to hiss a question to his wife. "What the fuck—"

She clutched his thigh, dug in her nails, and murmured, "Later."

Later needed to hurry its ass up.

The courses passed with interesting conversation, especially considering the guests all appeared human. But they spoke of the next blood moon, of combing the populace for the right kind of genes, of buying plane-loads of weapons.

And everyone treated him with deference. As in

they called him fucking "sir." A first for him, and after the initial shock, he quite enjoyed it.

The second offer came at the dessert table teeming with decadent sweets. Chris stood eyeing the promised mousse but then hesitating because there was also some crème brûlée on the table, the caramel topping on it crunchy.

Hard decisions that were interrupted by, "Greetings, Son of Perdition."

He turned to see a woman in her sixties to seventies, short, gray-haired, and wearing more jewels than an Egyptian pharaoh.

"Hey." Suave, because nothing said taking over the world more than a one-syllable reply.

"I know we are supposed to route our offers through your intermediary; however, I want you to know that my company can arm your legions."

"With?" he asked.

"Anything you like. Guns, knives, flamethrowers, grenades."

Toys! He almost clapped his hands in delight. He negotiated instead. "That's cool." Like him. He shrugged. "And what do you want in return? A condo on the Styx? A townhouse in the inner ring?"

To his surprise, she shook her head. "No need for reward. I offer everything I have to the next King of Hell. The Atheos stand ready to serve." She lifted her long gown enough to give him a peek at her ankles, which were trim in defiance of her age, but of more interest was the tattoo there. A burning pentagram with a triple six in the center. His symbol.

How cool. And she wasn't the only one wearing it he soon realized.

As a child, when he was the focus of a cult that had worshipped the Antichrist, he'd often seen the symbol, but he'd never realized it extended outside that smallish group.

Once he began looking around, he noticed many in attendance wearing it on ankles, and the insides of wrists. One man had it behind his ear, and it only showed when he turned a certain way and his hair parted. Others wore pins shaped in his mark.

It did a lot for a man's ego to realize the cult he'd thought lost, extended around the world.

He accepted two more offers of aid before he managed to head back to Isobel bearing two dessert plates. He set them down, and she remarked, "I already got a treat."

He tossed her a droll smile. "Hate to break it to you, but these are for me."

"I know. Which is why this is so much fun." She took her finger and jabbed it down into the hard surface of the crème brûlée, cracking it. Then she licked it, her lithe, pink tongue reminding him of her oral expertise, and all was forgiven.

"Do that again," he encouraged, sliding his mousse over.

"Perv," she said with affection.

In between bites, he decided to tell Isobel about his conversation with the old lady. "Just had something weird happen while I was getting dessert."

"Weirder than this dinner? I thought I'd met all of Mother's friends, but I don't know a face in this bunch."

"You wouldn't unless your mother was an Atheos."

"What's an atheos?"

"It's Latin for atheist, and it's what those who belong to the cult of the Antichrist call themselves."

"I thought they were called Satanists."

He shook his head. "No. Those are the people who worship my dad. The Atheos worship no god."

"But you're the son of one."

"Not really. Most people don't consider Lucifer a god. He is the Devil. Totally different thing."

"Potato, po-tah-toe," she said.

"Hey, you asked."

"What are your minions saying that's got you perplexed?"

Chris leaned close enough to murmur against her lobe. "Can you explain why someone would say I had an intermediary?"

"What?" Isobel paused with a spoonful of chocolate cake inches from her mouth.

"Intermediary. As in someone taking offers to add soldiers to my legion."

"You don't say." Isobel's head turned, and he caught her staring at her mother. Marya, who'd arrived shortly after the soiree began, looked quite resplendent, a true dame of the ball. The diamonds at her ears, neck, and on her fingers sparkled, sharp as the smile tugging her lips.

"You don't think..." He didn't even bother finishing the thought. His mother-in-law surely wasn't interested in helping him build an army. Was she?

"I do think," she said grimly. "And I want to know why." Isobel rose, only to have Chris yank her down.

"Don't leave." Panic fluttered in his chest. An urge to comb his hair hit him hard. A teeth check wouldn't be amiss either.

"What's wrong?" his wife asked.

How could she ask? Did she not sense the coming apocalypse?

"Don't you see her?" Dressed in a long, burgundy velvet gown, the neckline high, the sleeves long, the shape of it flaring and ruffled.

"See who?"

Ominous music began to play—Ligeti's *Requiem*—just in time to greet the arrival of... "My mother."

14

His mother was here?

"Where?" Isobel glanced over to where Chris stared and noticed just a bunch of people. Humans as far as she could tell, all sporting the same tattoo, wearing the same manic expressions. Despite the different clothes, and being from varying parts of the world, it wasn't hard to guess that they were part of a club. The I-worship-the-Antichrist club.

Since I married him, does that mean I need a tattoo, as well?

"She's over there," Chris hissed. "In the burgundy dress."

Isobel glanced again. Saw only one person who matched the description.

"That's your mom?" Skepticism laced her words. The woman of whom he spoke looked quite prim and proper. Her hands were folded over her stomach as she stood demurely, not making any kind of waves. She didn't have a crown of thorns or a slave on a leash. No ominous cloud surrounded her.

Kind of disappointing.

"It's her. We need to leave. Now."

She put her hand on his arm to stop him from rising. "Don't be so melodramatic. She's obviously here for a reason."

"Death and annihilation."

"Or maybe she thought it would be a nice public setting for her to truly meet her son for the first time." Isobel fed him a calming line while mentally freaking out. *His mom is here.* Her mother-in-law, a possible goddess just returned from another dimension. An unknown force who'd tried to keep them apart. *Because she hates me.* What if she'd shown up to rectify his marriage?

Would Chris turn into a mama's boy and ditch her?

Over my dead body. She stood.

"Where are you going?" he hissed. "I thought you said we weren't going to run."

"We're not. I'm going to say hello. You coming?"

He stared at her, the struggle in him visible. "You're kidding, right?"

"Not really. She's obviously here for a reason."

"Did you miss the part where I said she probably wants to kill us all?"

"Dressed like that? Doubtful. Let's go say hi."

He frowned, but behind it, she could see the longing. This was his mother. The woman who'd spent considerable energy trying to communicate with Chris while imprisoned. He owed it to himself to at least meet her.

"What if she bites?" he said, still hesitating.

"Bite her back." She grabbed him by the hand and tugged him to his feet. Keeping her eye on the prize, and a hand latched on to Chris, she edged her way to the other end of the dining hall, past bodies who'd stopped to chat, dodging plates and glasses held aloft.

They rounded the corner of the table and a clear space. Isobel got to see her mother-in-law up close. The black eyes. As in no whites whatsoever. Must make it hard to blend in with the general populace.

Isobel flashed a smile that her mother had made her practice during her lessons on good manners.

It wasn't returned.

"You. You're the daughter of that wizard."

Isobel stumbled as a voice spoke disparagingly within her mind.

"To think you're married to my son instead of someone truly worthy of him."

The plain truth of it struck at her insecurities.

"You should end it now. Stop causing this misery. Do the right thing. For once."

"Stop that, Mother," Chris snapped.

The words caused Isobel to flinch, blink, and then stare slack-jawed. "She— Uh." It would sound crazy if spoken aloud.

But Chris understood. "She's trying to worm her way inside and play with your doubts. Don't let her."

How? How exactly did one stop an attack on one's mind? She did the only thing she could think of. Sang the baby bumble bee song inside her head.

The grimace on his mother's face resulted in a flood of relief that left her lightheaded. The attack had stopped for the moment, but just in case it was temporary, she kept her mind humming while they approached the woman.

Chris stopped a few feet from the other woman. "Mother." The word was flat.

"No hug?" she asked, a silver brow quirking.

Isobel couldn't blame him for staying back. The chill emanating from the woman didn't encourage close contact.

"What are you doing here?" he asked

"I came to see you, of course, since you couldn't be bothered."

Having been the recipient of many a guilt trip, Isobel recognized it, but she could see Chris's expression twist. Part guilt, part confusion.

"This isn't the time or place for a family reunion," he stated.

"When is it time, my son? I waited while in my prison for you to make contact. I tolerated you rebuffing my attempts."

"Attempts? You possessed dead bodies and came after me!"

"Only because I had no other recourse. Things have changed now. I'm no longer a prisoner."

"But you're still causing shit."

"Language." His mother frowned in disapproval, and Chris opened his mouth, probably to apologize.

Isobel jumped in. "Would you like a glass of wine? Dinner is over, but we have dessert."

The glare aimed her way had Isobel sidling closer to Chris. His mother snapped, "No one gave you permission to speak."

"Don't talk to my wife like that," Chris said with a glower. "You need to leave."

"Leave?" His mother laughed, a discordant jangle —and somewhere, a demon got its wings. "But I've only just arrived, and your future commanders need to see we are a united front."

"United front for what?"

"For what is to come. We have to secure their armies for the coming battle."

"What battle?" he asked, his expression intent. "And what makes you think I'd work with you? I hate you."

"Emotions are a waste of time. The sooner you learn to shun them, the easier you'll find it to make the right decisions."

"Bite me," he snapped.

Isobel found it interesting to note that, despite the heated discussion, no one around them paid them any mind. On the contrary, it was as if they were contained in a clear bubble. People flowed around them without interruption or even a direct stare. *As if we're invisible.*

A very practical kind of magic. Only she saw no magic. Felt no threads.

How was that possible? She tuned back to Chris and his mother, arguing heatedly, like a typical mother and son. Hunh. Imagine that.

"This is *my* evening," he stated rather emphatically. "These people came to meet me and pledge their allegiance to me. Not you."

"You wouldn't even be here if it weren't for me," Mama Antichrist declared.

Disdain curled his lip. "Is this going to turn into some sob story about how you gained a ton of weight while pregnant and I had a fat head and your body was never the same?"

"A gigantic head that took four stitches. Do you know how much those threads of fate cost me?" His mother lifted her chin. "You owe me."

"You can kiss my—"

Isobel jumped in. "Listen, Mac." Shorter form of Mother Antichrist. "You'll have to give Chris some time. He's been a tad overwhelmed lately."

"Doing what? Digging holes. Playing games on his phone." Mac crossed her arms. "It is time he stopped his childish pursuits and took over his responsibilities as a man."

"And what responsibilities are those exactly?"

Isobel asked, stepping in front of Chris when he muttered, "I'll show you who's a man."

"He needs to stop running from his destiny."

"I am not destroying the world," Chris declared.

"That is only one option," his mother replied. "You seem to forget the other one where you rule Hell instead."

"There's only one King of Hell," boomed a voice, startling Isobel. "And that's me!"

"You!" Mac went from cold and very bitchy mom-face to colder, really pissed ex-girlfriend baby mama.

"Yes, me. And you are?" Lucifer tucked his hands behind his back, his suit a rather sedate gray, his tie a mauve swirl that complemented the flower in his lapel —the bloom opened and blinked, the center yawning to show several rows of tiny, sharp teeth. Gaia must have dressed him.

"Do not pretend you don't know who I am," spat Mac.

"Scullery maid?" Lucifer asked.

"Don't play stupid. It's my mom, asshole." Chris's face turned an unhealthy shade of red, and smoke began to steam from his nose.

"Morgana?" Lucifer asked as he eyed her up and down. "You did not age well."

"You should know better than to judge an outer shell." In the blink of an eye, the old woman turned young, her body a shapely hourglass, her dark hair hinting of blue highlights. The eyes remained the same dark pits. "Is that better?"

Lucifer squinted. "You're all right, I guess. Still a bitch, though, I see."

"Don't you call her names." Poor Chris. Caught defending the woman he hated to the man he hated more.

"What else should I call her? She's been a right pain in my ass lately. Causing me all kinds of extra work."

"Did it ever occur to you she might've had a good reason?" Chris retorted, while Mac—ahem, Morgana—looked on, her lips curved into a smug smile. "After all, you did knock her up and then lock her away."

"For being bad," Lucifer explained.

"But bad is what I do best." The woman lifted a brow.

"Says you. I don't recall us fucking at all." Lucifer shrugged and said in an aside to Isobel, "It was the first time Gaia and I broke up. I spent quite a lot of time drunk on my ass. I banged a ton of chicks." He turned back to Morgana. "You mustn't have been real good at it since I don't remember."

It was like he'd slapped her in the face.

"Why...you..." Steam began to rise from her skin as if she boiled from within. Morgana's hair started to twist and lift, carried on an invisible breeze. Her features took on a gaunt cast, the cheeks hollowing, her skin darkening as if a shadow were being cast.

And Lucifer, the smartass, kept going. "Nope, still not familiar. Why don't you hike that dress and purse those other lips at me? Maybe then you'll jiggle a memory loose."

The woman in the burgundy grown expanded, Morgana's features and body distorting into a misty version, a veritable cloud of smoke.

Now people in the room took notice.

"Stop that," Isobel hissed.

"Stop what?" Lucifer asked. "Just telling the truth. You should be congratulating me. I didn't think I had the ability to speak the truth, and yet, here I am, explaining to the mother of my child that she meant so little to me that I don't remember a fucking thing."

If a mist could scream, this one did, a piercing shriek that went on and on, the wrongness of it hitting the ears like an icepick. People dropped to their knees, clutching at their heads.

Isobel could understand their pain. It pinched her something fierce.

Moisture dripped from her nose. She reached to touch, and the tips of her fingers came away wet and red. She hit the ground on her knees and, through a cloud, heard Chris yelling for her.

Hands gripped her, and his voice cut through the noise. "Don't listen to her." Then a warm cocoon of air surrounded her, cutting off the sound. The relief sent her into oblivion.

15

Losing consciousness, Isobel hit the floor, her face bloody, her breathing ragged. An attempted murder of his wife.

Chris lost his fucking mind.

"Stop it," he yelled at this mother.

But she continued to shriek, her misty body spreading out, an ominous cloud of doom.

As for Lucifer, he did his best to encourage Morgana's deadly cry. "Still not ringing any bells, Morgana. Are you sure you didn't molest me while I was unconscious? It wouldn't be the first time it happened," he confided to Chris.

Mother screamed some more.

Chris felt the rage in him growing as he took in the scene of devastation on what should have been a night of triumph.

The people in the room twitched on the floor.

With the exception of Rasputin, who scowled beside his daughter, Marya, a glowing red nimbus surrounding their bodies.

They were protected, but what of everyone else? Those pledged to him, gone. With his powers now back, he saw their souls fleeing, not far given Charon and his boatmen had a ticket for them across the Styx.

And what of his wife? She lay prone on the floor, a golden halo around her. Magic protected her, but for how long? Would she recover from the damage she'd suffered? And more importantly, how dare his mother cause her harm.

How. Dare. She?

"Enough!" he boomed, casting out his hands, feeling the magic rushing, fueled by his ire, his frustration.

As if a gag were shoved in her annoying, misty mouth, Mother stopped her infernal screeching, and silence descended.

He glared at her smoky body. "If I didn't hate you before, I do now. You can forget us becoming allies. Ever." No one hurt his duckie. No. One.

"You will need my help in the coming battle."

"Fuck you, and fuck your battle. Fight alone. See if I care. Actually, after what you've done, you can count on me fighting against you."

"You need me," the wraith said, the cool words brushing against his skin.

"No, what I need is my wife. Alive. And you just tried to kill her."

"Not very effectively," Lucifer added. At Chris's glare, he spread his hands and said, "What? It's the truth. Just saying, if I was going to murder some people, they wouldn't still be drawing breath."

"I'm going to choke you if you don't shut the fuck up," Chris snapped. "And as for you." He directed his mighty glare on his cloudy mother. "I want nothing to do with you. Nothing. Leave. And don't fucking come back."

"Yeah, what he said," Lucifer taunted.

"You," the mist breathed. "You are the bane of my existence. The reason for my vengeance. And the worst part is..." The fog swirled around Lucifer, and her last words were whispered, "I don't remember being with you either."

Then the mist was gone.

Lucifer gaped. "Doesn't remember me?" the Devil sputtered. "Impossible. I am the greatest screw she ever had. The mightiest of lovers. The biggest serpent that ever slithered into her hole. The—"

"Would you shut the fuck up," Chris snapped. "I really don't care right now that you're a piss-poor screw. Isobel is hurt."

Actually, just about everyone in the room was injured, the bodies on the floor still not moving. The only thing that kept him from losing it completely was the fact that Isobel still drew breath. But her skin was ashen. The blood a stark reminder of her injury.

"Ah, for fuck's sake. Your mother is right. You've got to stop letting your emotions cloud your judgment."

"She's my wife," he growled. "I love her."

"Then fix her."

"I'm not a bloody doctor."

"No, you're a fucking Baphomet. With magic inside you. Use it."

"How?"

"What do you mean, how? You just fucking used some on your mother."

"Because I was mad."

"Which only amplified it. It's still there. In you. Use it. Don't think about how. Do you think about how you breathe?"

"No."

"Because it's instinct, my boy."

Instinct? His predispositions usually led him astray. But in this instance, he couldn't doubt. He knelt beside his wife, her skin pale, the blood too bright. Her life...

He could see it pulsing only weakly inside her. He reached through the golden shield around her. It dissipated, and he touched her skin. Rubbed the tips of his fingers against her body then closed his eyes. He called to his magic.

Come here.

His father made a noise. "Don't ask. Control it. Take it. Make it your bitch."

The words roused his anger, which, in turn, pumped him. He didn't just pull; he yanked in some power and then imagined blowing it into his wife.

He gasped as he felt it siphoning from him into her.

Isobel sucked in a deep breath. Then another.

"Keep going. You fixed her spirit. Now go after the broken bits inside the body."

Chris almost asked what his father meant, but then he felt it. Felt the magic entering her veins, spreading through her body until it found a tear. It knitted it together then moved on, mending each of the rips it found.

"All done now. Pull out before you overload that brain of hers."

With a hiccup of breath, Chris yanked away and slapped his hands on his thighs. He panted as if he'd run a race. Sweated as if he'd actually exerted his body.

And still, Isobel lay unmoving on the floor.

"Why isn't she waking?" he asked.

Lucifer crouched alongside and ran his hand over her body. "You fixed what was wrong, but her body and mind still need time to recover. Give her a bit of sleep, and she'll be riding your cock again in no time."

"Promise?" Chris knew better than to take the Devil at his word, but if he made it binding...

"Are you calling me a liar?" The slap on his back

almost sent him toppling. "Smart boy. Must take after me and not your hag of a mother."

"Isobel!" Marya screeched as she dropped to her knees beside her daughter.

Chris relinquished his wife to her worried mother and stood facing off against his father.

"Say it. Promise Isobel will be okay." Make it a promise. Take away the fear crushing his heart.

"Argh, today's youth. Just no respect for their elders. Fine. I promise she'll be fine. From this injury at any rate. But I would advise you to keep her away from Morgana. She always did have a wicked temper on her."

"So you *do* remember her?"

"I have a vague recollection of the witch. Apparently, I should have heeded Merlin's warning. Damned Hell grog. It's made more than one demon wake up with an empty sac and an urge to throw up when he saw what he'd fucked."

"So you do know her," Chris said, trying to clarify.

"Maybe. Like I said, it's kind of foggy. Don't remember much about those years. But I recall the stories. Rumor had it she banged a lot of soldiers back in the day."

His father's crassness suddenly tired him. "Go away."

"I will, but not because you asked. Bloody Morgana ruined my Friday night by massacring a room full of people that, given their crimes, will need special processing. Now I have to work. Fucking Hell." With a snap of his fingers, a portal opened, and Lucifer stepped through, leaving behind a whiff of brimstone and falling ash.

His words, though, had Chris surveying the room anew. He noted Rasputin moving through the slumped bodies, nudging them with his foot, shaking his head and tugging his long beard.

"Are they all dead?" Chris asked.

"Very," the wizard reported grimly. "Hope you brought a shovel."

He hadn't, but the garden shed had one. He could use the mindless work. He changed before he began digging a mass grave for the bodies while Marya tended to an unconscious Isobel.

She'll be fine.

You're going to believe the Devil?

Better than the alternative. Wondering if she would die.

Why'd you do it, Mother?

Why had his mother killed everyone? They'd promised their aid. He would have had his army.

Yet, with one temper tantrum, she'd taken it all away.

I thought you wanted me to rule the world.

No reply.

Nothing but the sound of dirt being flung, the grunts as he exerted himself, the snick of the blade of the shovel digging into the ground.

The whisper of wings as something alighted and watched.

He lifted his head to see an angel perched on a tree branch, wings tucked behind his back, his blue gaze unblinking. Given it wasn't the first time, Chris didn't freak. But he did wish for a gun. A cookbook published in Hell—*The Joy of Cooking My Enemies*—claimed they tasted like pheasant when roasted.

"You do realize I can see you," Chris remarked, figuring he'd hold off on hunting the angel for the moment, especially since this one seemed more intent on watching than trying to earn brownie points by killing the Antichrist.

"There is still time. Time to repent. Time to change the future." The melodic words caused a shiver.

And a frown. "Shouldn't you be telling my mom that? I'm not the one causing shit."

"Morgana won't listen to reason. However, you... you can still make things right."

Pausing for a moment, Chris leaned on his shovel and stared at the angel, "Listen, bud—"

"I am Raphael."

"Listen, Ralphie, I'm not the one who's causing all kinds of trouble. Blame my mom." He'd been doing that for a while. "Who do you think is responsible for this?" He waved at the stack of bodies.

"She works to benefit you."

"Don't you blame this on me. I was perfectly happy with my life. I didn't ask for any of this."

"You're the Antichrist." Boldly spoken because it was the truth.

"What if I am? It's just a name. In case you weren't paying attention, I haven't done shit. I've not been going around murdering people or starting wars. Hell, I haven't even shoplifted anything lately." More to piss off his dad, who hated it every time he paid for something and left a tip.

"The words of the prophecy—"

"Can bite me. Last I heard, there was this thing called free will, and I plan to use it. Also, before you judge me, whatever happened to innocent until proven guilty? How you gonna condemn me for something I haven't even done?" Yet.

Raphael jumped to the ground, landing lightly on his slippered feet, his height more impressive now that they were face-to-face. "Once you've committed to your course, it will be too late. We have to cease the possibility right now."

It occurred to him that Ralphie was alone. Super odd, given that Chris knew the angels usually roamed in packs. "Why are you here?" he suddenly asked. "Did God send you?"

"Our Lord is tending to other matters."

"He has no idea you're here, and neither do your buddies."

"I undertook this mission alone to plead with you to do the right thing."

Chris leaned on his shovel and drawled, "What is the 'right thing?' Killing myself?"

"I would never ask someone to commit such a sin."

"Wouldn't ask, and yet what other choice is there? Tell me, Ralphie, what am I supposed to do? Tonight, I did nothing. Nothing at all. And still, people wanted to pledge themselves to me."

"They died for their promise."

"They didn't die because of me."

"Not directly, and yet the common link is you."

Chris began tipping the bodies into the hole. *Thunk, thud, squish.* "Don't blame me for the actions of others. I am not my mother. She has her own game. I have nothing to do with it."

"Then prove it. Renounce her. Forsake your father. Pledge yourself to repent and pay penance."

Pausing in his burial, Chris gaped at him. "Repent for what? Being fucking born? Are you fucking kidding me?"

"This is not a humorous matter, progeny of Lucifer."

"I'm not fucking laughing. But I'm also not repenting or dying or anything else either. Not for you, your god, or anyone. I have just as much right to live as the next man."

"Is that your final answer, Son of Perdition?"

"You can tell God and all your angelic brothers that I am not going to roll over. I might not know what my future holds, but I'll damned well be the one in charge of it. Not some prophecy by long-dead farts."

"You've been warned." With that final ominous statement, Raphael sprang into the air, his white wings unfurling and then flapping as he took off, taking his sanctimonious attitude with him.

"Prick," Chris muttered.

"Actually," said a new voice, that of his cousin, who came sauntering out of the shadows. "He has none. Dick, that is. The extremely devoted voluntarily make themselves eunuchs so they might better serve my father without the distraction of lust."

"He cut off his dick?" Chris shuddered. "That's just wrong."

"What did he want?" Jesus asked, heading to the edge of the pit and looking down.

"For me to hand myself over and basically renounce everything."

"It won't stop what's to come."

"Kind of what I said." Chris began to dump dirt on the bodies. "What are you doing here? I didn't know the mother-in-law invited you."

"She didn't. However, a little bird told me there was trouble. I arrived too late."

"You missed a visit from my mother."

"I take it, it didn't go well?

Chris arched a brow. "Did the bodies give it away?"

"Isobel is alive?"

"I'd be laying waste to the world if she wasn't," he grumbled.

"You do realize your mother might try to kill her again."

"Yeah." His mommy had issues.

"What are you going to do about it?" Jesus kept yapping and asking questions but didn't offer any solutions.

Pity, Chris could have used an idea. "Dunno." Short of killing someone who couldn't be killed, what could he do?

As if reading his mind, Jesus said, "Now that your mother is on the mortal plane, it might be possible to destroy her."

"How? Because my understanding is, she can't be killed, which is why Merlin and my dad locked her away."

"That happened centuries ago. We've gotten better weapons since then."

Could one of them truly kill his mom? It shouldn't have caused a pang, but it did. Still, what choice did she leave him?

"Are you offering to take care of Morgana?" Calling her his mom while discussing her murder seemed cold even by his standards.

"Not me, but I can arm some people."

"Don't you mean angels?"

Jesus nodded. "But I need your help. You need to lure Morgana out into the open."

Betray his mom to save Isobel and maybe the world?

Rather than reply, he indicated the other shovel.

Jesus grimaced but rolled up his sleeves and grabbed it. Together, the sons of God and the Devil buried bodies in a backyard under the waning moon while Isobel remained unconscious in bed.

While Chris wondered if he could lead his mother into a trap. Kill the woman who'd birthed him.

Would it save the world?

Would it save him?

And if he failed? What would happen then?

16

Foot dangling off the armrest of the chair, Bambi awaited the return of her father. She'd been summoned into his mighty presence and knew better than to leave before talking to Daddy Dear.

Not that she ever called him "Daddy" to his face. Only Muriel ever survived that privilege. Most of the time, the Devil preferred to pretend he had no progeny. Kids made him feel old. The fact that he'd come into existence at the dawn of humanity never even entered his mental process.

But despite his gruff exterior, she could comfort herself with the fact that he didn't completely ignore her as he did some of his other daughters. All dead now. It wasn't easy being Lucifer's kid. People tried to use them to get to their father. Threatened them if he didn't comply.

Father never gave in to terrorists or blackmail. He

did, however, punish them later. Cold comfort to the siblings who perished.

Since his involvement with Gaia, and the advent of decent birth control, Lucifer no longer fathered any bastards at all, which meant Bambi only had Muriel left for family—and her recently discovered brother, Chris. Although, given Chris's actions, she wouldn't wager he'd live long.

He seemed intent on doing his best to poke the Devil. At some point, the Devil would poke back—with a sharpened stake.

Speaking of, the Devil arrived wearing a scowl, smoke pouring from his ears. "Fuck me! This is not what I'd planned to do tonight."

Noting his suit, which lacked any kind of outrageous color or animal print, she couldn't help but remark, "You're looking awfully respectable. Who were you trying to impress?"

Lucifer glared down at his ensemble. "Gaia. She hid my duckies on me. And my sharks. She got rid of all my custom-made outfits, even the sailor suit."

Thank you, Gaia. "Is that why you look pissed?"

"No, I'm pissed because what was supposed to be a fun evening of taunting and mayhem has now turned into a working one. Damnable woman. She killed them all."

"Killed who, my lord?" This was one of the times where she needed to be more the employee than the daughter.

"The guests at Christopher's party."

"My brother had a party and didn't invite me?" She scowled. "That little fucker. And after all the times I helped him."

"While I'd usually tell you to hate on him, this wasn't actually his fault. His mother-in-law arranged it, and it was more business meeting than party, really. Bunch of bigwigs from around the world who wanted to pledge their allegiance to the Antichrist and all that shit. Which is dumb, considering their sins mean their souls belong to me already."

"Is that why you killed them?" she asked, trying to understand.

"Not me. *Her*."

"Her...who?"

"Morgana, his mother."

Bambi blinked her extra-long lashes—all-natural, and at great cost. "His mom showed up? How did that happen? I thought that spell you cast was supposed to keep them apart."

"It did. For a while. But the bastard might be a touch stronger than I gave him credit for. The spell I placed on him is completely gone now. Every single layer of magical protection—poof!" Lucifer smacked his palms together, the sound echoing like an explosion. "Which means that his hag of a mother can find him anytime she likes."

"Which is bad?"

"Depends on which side of it you're on. For me?

Very bad. Because now that they're reuniting, we won't be able to stop it," Lucifer grumbled. "This will mean the end of my reign and chaos on Earth.

"Kind of melodramatic, don't you think?"

"Don't mock me. This is a catastrophe."

"Are you sure? Because you also claimed calamity when Cook ran out of maple syrup."

"You have no idea how close it came then," he muttered. "And now, we're even more fucked."

"Can you rewind and explain exactly what happened at this party that's got you in a tizzy?"

"Take a gander for yourself."

He waved a hand, and an opaque disk stretched and hung itself midair, acting as a screen.

She watched what appeared to be a rather stuffy dinner, attended by her brother, Chris, and his wife.

"Looks boring," she remarked.

"Wait for it." The scene sped forward, and Bambi noted the confrontation between Chris and an older woman. Lucifer arrived, and the old broad turned hot.

Bambi poked the image to pause it. "Did I hear you correctly when you said her name was Morgana? We're not talking *the* Morgana, are we?"

"Yes, that Morgana. Le Fay. In the flesh. Pissed-off flesh, I might add."

"Pissed because you locked her up."

"Because she gave us no other choice."

"Us being?"

"Me, Merlin, and my brother."

She blinked in disbelief.

Lucifer shrugged. "It might not happen often, but Elyon and I occasionally work toward a common goal."

"In this case, the common goal being locking way a pregnant woman. What exactly did she do that was so bad?"

"Went on a rampage with her horsemen. Caused all kinds of death, which, in turn, meant a shit-ton of work for me. Dark days," he said with a glower. "She had to be stopped."

"But she was pregnant."

"So she claimed. At the time, I would have sworn it wasn't mine."

Even Bambi had to cringe at his coldness in incarcerating a pregnant woman. But this was Morgana Le Fay, the strongest witch ever known to man. Imprisoning her was merciful compared to other—more permanent—options of removal.

Rebuking her father wouldn't serve any purpose. Instead, she poked the vision, and it continued playing, showing Morgana turning into a smoky wraith, bodies dropping to the floor, including Isobel.

She leaned close and studied the image. "Is everyone dead?"

"Everyone in that room died, except the Rasputins and your brother. Those outside, having a cigarette or fooling around in the bushes, who missed her banshee cry were slaughtered by the horsemen who snuck onto the property."

"I assume they weren't godly men and women?"

"Not even fucking close. All of them despots and murderers and corporate magnates, the worst criminals of all. Which means, I'll need to process them myself."

Bambi leaned back. "And that's why you're pissed? It's not that big of a deal. You were going to get their souls sooner or later."

"Yeah, but I wasn't expecting every one of those dead leaders pledged to Christopher's cause to join them at the same time," he grumbled.

"You lost me again."

"The dinner was a power move by Marya, Isobel's mum. Bloody witch invited all the Atheos in power so they could meet the Antichrist and give him an army."

Chris made a power play? No wonder Daddy was pissed. "Now that their leaders are dead, doesn't that make the deal null and void?"

"No. Because the soldiers have joined their leaders in Hell."

"All of them?" Bambi's eyes widened. "But how?"

"Pestilence, Famine, and Death have been busy sowing their seeds around the world. Thousands upon thousands have died this night. With thousands more expected tomorrow and the day after."

"Does Chris know?"

"Does it matter? It has begun. We are moving toward the final battle."

"What does that mean?" she asked.

He shrugged. "Fuck if I know. The seers never see past the fight itself. Just the events leading up to it."

"What are you going to do?"

"Pack my suitcase and call it a day."

Bambi gaped. "You're leaving?"

"Yup. I am not in the mood to deal with the end of the world."

"What about your minions? Hell?" She knew better than to ask about her own wellbeing. Daddy liked those who helped themselves—especially if they did it without paying. The King of Lies was also the king of dine and dash.

Lucifer tucked his hands behind his back. "Usually, I would say fuck it, but being a reformed man because of my hot wife, I actually have a plan."

Given the glint in his eyes and the smirk on his lips, Bambi wouldn't like it.

"What are you going to do?"

"More like, who am I going to screw?" Lucifer laughed. But no one laughed with him.

When she heard his plan, she could only shake her head. "This won't end well."

"That's what I've been saying. If I were you, daughter, I'd plan an extended vacation elsewhere."

Leave? While not the most altruistic person, Bambi did have some lines.

"We have to tell Muriel."

"Already did. She thinks I am overreacting."

"Are you?" The Devil could be a bit of a drama llama.

"Time will tell."

"If there is such a notion as time when all is said and done," she grumbled.

"Such pessimism. Don't you have any faith at all?"

"No. You told me faith was for morons and to sell them fake holy water and then watch as vampires eat them."

"That's brilliant." Lucifer grinned, with too many teeth. "I really should write a book. *The Devil's Guide to Common Fucking Sense.* Maybe I'll do that once I retire."

Yes, retire, because the Devil's brilliant plan was to let someone else take over his job.

CHRIS GAPED at his dad and blurted, "Me? You want me to rule over Hell?"

Of course, that wasn't how the conversation had started. It began with, "Dirty peeping motherfucker," when Chris noticed the old goat at the foot of the bed, leering at him and Isobel.

No knock, because that would imply manners.

No warning, because that was how the Devil rolled.

"Is that lazy wife of yours still sleeping?" his dad asked.

"She's in a coma, asshole."

"Then wake her up. Give the girl a kiss. Or you could take a page from that delightfully decadent set of books Anne Rice wrote and try something a little kinkier."

"I am not molesting my wife while she's unconscious." Although he did find himself stroking her cheek more than once. It stunned him still to realize that he'd almost lost her.

Only Isobel, her mother, and her grandfather had survived. Of the dignitaries who'd promised him an army? All dead. Even the servants had croaked.

Thanks a lot, Mother. So much for finally building a legion of loyal troops. In one fell swoop, his mother had taken it all away, and the demon responsible had returned to cause more shit.

"If you're not willing to give the girl some tongue, then I guess I can weather Gaia's wrath and do it for you." Lucifer approached, and despite Isobel being dressed, Chris drew the covers to her neck and glared.

"Don't you dare touch her."

"You do realize that challenging someone as testosterone-charged as me almost guarantees I will do just that."

"Lay one finger on my wife, and I will find a way to kill you."

"If I hadn't made other plans, I'd be curious to see you try. Alas, I am expected elsewhere shortly."

"Then go."

The Devil seemed rather put-out. "Not going to ask me where I'm going?"

"Don't care."

"Of course, you do. I can see the curiosity burning bright inside you."

"The only thing I'm curious about is how far I can shove my foot up your ass."

"Farther than you'd expect. But we digress. I'm leaving," Lucifer announced.

"Good."

"As in leaving-leaving. Not only Earth, but Hell. But before I go, I need to put my affairs in order."

The claim drew Chris's attention. "What are you talking about?"

"I am talking about naming an heir. Someone to take over, to continue meting out the epic torture that Hell is known for."

An heir? Chris's momentary elation quickly deflated. "Let me guess, you've come to rub my face in the fact you chose Muriel to take over the family business."

Lucifer's face crinkled as he made a moue of displeasure. "Muriel? Take over Hell? But she's a girl."

"Since when do you care? You're always asking her for help." And yes, that might have emerged a little sulkier than he liked.

"I'm not the one asking. She keeps meddling in my affairs. Sticking her nose where it doesn't belong. Trying to show me up with her harem of lovers. I could have a harem, too, if Gaia weren't such a jealous shrew."

A female voice exclaimed from midair, "*Am not, you randy goat.*"

"Stop spying on me, wench. Can't you see I'm busy

chatting with my bastard son?" Lucifer shook his fist at the ceiling. "Anyhow, as I was saying, I'm looking for a replacement."

Even Chris had to admit the truth. "It should go to Muriel given she's the one who's done the most for Hell." Not because he couldn't have accomplished the same but because no one had asked him—and he had too much pride to offer.

"Giving it to a woman would be much too enlightened of me. I am not that progressive. No, I've decided to stick with tradition and leave it to my oldest male heir. This kind of a job needs someone with balls, the kind that hangs between the legs. And given my choices are rather limited; apparently, that's you."

Chris might have blinked a few times. He also jammed his finger in his ear and said, "Eh? What's that you said?"

"You. Are. My. Heir."

No mistaking the words this time. "Me. You're leaving Hell to me?"

"I'd leave it to my other son but, apparently, one can't leave it to the unborn." Way to remind Chris that he wasn't the first choice.

Still...ruler of Hell? "This is a trick." Chris frowned at the Devil. "What's the catch?"

"No catch. I'm leaving, the job is open, and I am handing over the reins to my empire."

"Without dying."

"That's the plan."

What of his scheme to kill his father? Then again, the only reason he'd contemplated killing Lucifer was so he could fulfill his destiny to become king. None of the prophecies specified how it would happen.

"What if I don't want it?"

A hearty chuckle erupted from his dad. "Ha. That's funny, boy. Not want it." Snicker. "We both know you covet my crown."

"I also want to see you dead and pushing up daisies."

"You know what the Rolling Stones say."

In this case, though, could he get what he wanted? King of Hell. It had a nice ring to it. But would he really be ruling it? What of his dad? Would he be meddling every chance he got? "Let's say I take the job, what will you be doing?"

"Hopefully, drinking something fruity on a beach in that lovely Atlantis dimension while rubbing suntan lotion on my wife's belly. It helps with her nausea, don't you know."

"So would divorcing you," Chris grumbled.

"Such a funny boy. I'll miss spying on your acerbic wit."

His dad thought him witty? "What about my mom?"

"What of her?"

Chris hadn't heard a peep since the disastrous party. He didn't know if that was a good or bad sign. Watching the news meant he caught glimpses of the havoc her horsemen wreaked, but the silence from her proved disturbing.

"What am I supposed to do about Mom?"

"How the fuck would I know? I tried locking Morgana away, and we all saw how well that went. By taking over my throne, you'll have all of Hell's resources at your fingertips. Surely, you can handle one woman."

"She's not just a woman." Morgana, according to Rasputin, was the most powerful sorceress ever conceived on Earth. No one quite knew how she'd gotten her magic or strength. Her apparent immortality was also a mystery, but her madness...proven fact and not something he was keen on dealing with.

"She's your mother. With me gone, perhaps she'll forget her vendetta and behave. Just be the son she always wanted."

"How? By drawing her a fucking picture to put on her fridge?"

"Or give her something else to focus on." Lucifer cast a glance on Isobel. "Or someone new."

"I am not using my wife to placate my mother."

"Not your wife, idiot. A child. A grandchild. Plant a seed in her belly if you haven't already. Hard to tell," Lucifer said with a frown.

The very idea of Isobel carrying his child—*my very own son!*—slammed him in the gut. And Lucifer didn't give him time to recover.

"Nice chatting with you. Not." The Devil chuckled. "Now that we've settled things, *adios, amigo.*"

"When do you leave for the beach?"

"As soon as I grab my suitcase. Can't tarry. I want to make sure I get a good spot before it comes."

"What comes?"

"The end of the world, of course. It's nigh. And I, for one, plan to have an awesome seat to watch."

Snap. With a click of his fingers, Lucifer disappeared, leaving Chris to wonder if he'd imagined the encounter.

Yet the smell of brimstone and ash hung in the air, and the cloven hoof marks singed into the light blue carpet said it had happened.

Still, his father had to be lying about leaving him Hell. He couldn't just abdicate like that.

Could he?

He sat back alongside Isobel, his weight causing the mattress to dip, and sighed.

"My lord needs something."

He stiffened. "Who said that?"

"It is I, my lord. Your most humble servant, at your service."

Servant? But they'd all died in the dinner party incident, and Marya had yet to replace them.

Chris glanced over his shoulder and saw a strange creature—short, bald, his skin showing a green pallor.

Chris jumped to his feet. "Who the fuck are you?"

"Philokrates."

"*What* are you?" was his next question because he'd never seen the likes of this dude.

"I am a majordomo."

"In English?"

The green fellow sighed. "What is it with today's youth, lacking in the niceties? Let me put this in a way you'll understand, then. Think of me as the Alfred of the Underworld. The butler from Hell."

"Why are you here? Shouldn't you be in Hell?" With the rest of the ugly demons.

If Alfred had brows, they would have hit the top of his forehead. "We are in the Pit, my lord. We have been since the moment the previous Dark Lord transferred his glorious reign to his heir."

"You mean it's true?"

"You are Hell's King," announced the gnomish servant.

Chris blinked. Looked for some words to speak. Failed.

Isobel chose that moment to rouse, her lashes fluttering, her gaze falling on Alfred, her voice groggy as she said, "Did you feed the Mogwai after midnight?"

"He's not a gremlin. This is—um, how do you say it again?" he asked.

"Philokrates."

A mouthful. "He's our butler, and he says we're in Hell."

Isobel rose to her elbows and smirked. "Given

we're under my mom's roof, that's probably an accurate assessment."

"Ahem. If I might interject, my lady, while the room might appear identical to that which you inhabited on the earthly plane, we are most definitely in the Hell dimension. You can glance out the windows if you'd like."

Chris did like. He strode over to the curtains and flung them open, only to gape.

He'd seen Hell before. His longest visit being in a cell his father had kept him in before using him as a pawn. So he was vaguely familiar with the place. But he'd never been a guest of the castle.

The view proved unlike any other. The window hung high in the air, lofty enough that he could see out over the city, the buildings—a jagged collection of dusty stone and rusted metal teeth—forming a line beyond the castle.

From their spot in the turret, he glanced down to see a vast courtyard, the cobblestones a reddish gray with a path in the dust, leading to a massive wrought iron gate, red with rust and manned by hulking creatures wearing horned helmets and carrying long spears.

"We really are in the castle," he mused aloud. But how? He'd never even felt the transition. Would have never even guessed. The magic involved... *How did he do it?* And more importantly, how could Chris hope to even come close to filling his father's cloven shoes?

"Why are we in the Pit?" Isobel asked, leaving the bed to come and stand beside him.

He couldn't reply. Couldn't say it aloud because it sounded so preposterous.

Alfred did it for him.

"Because Christopher Percy Baphomet the first has been declared Hell's King."

Eep.

18

―――――――

"Slap me," Isobel said.

"What?" Chris exclaimed.

"Pinch me. Goose me. Something to wake me up, because I think the gremlin over there just said you were Hell's King."

"Yeah. I kind of am."

"All hail the new Dark Lord!" exclaimed the green minion.

"Did you kill your father while I was passed out?" she asked.

"No."

"Did your mother tear out his entrails and choke him with them?" Which, given the last thing she recalled involved Lucifer taunting Morgana, was highly likely.

"Nope, but that would have been enjoyable."

"Did he die in battle?"

"I wish. But no, he's not dead. On the contrary, he is very much alive, just not here anymore. And before you ask, he came to see me, said he was retiring, and handed me the job, then left on vacation with Gaia."

"He left Hell to you?" Then, despite knowing he'd be pissed, she had to ask. "Are you sure he wanted you to have it and not Muriel?" She almost winced saying it aloud, yet Chris didn't take offense.

"I asked him the same thing but, apparently, because he's sexist and I'm the only family member with a dong, I am the one stuck with it."

"My husband is Hell's King. Hunh." Isobel frowned. "I kind of expected more." A mighty battle. Definitely some death. Angst, by Chris, who wouldn't want to kill his father but would because of fate pulling strings. This quiet reassignment seemed... "How boring."

"No shit. He didn't even stick around to show me the ropes. Just...the job is yours. And then, *bam*, he was gone."

Which meant, there was a catch. There had to be.

She whirled on the gremlin. "You. Short, green guy."

"Philokrates."

"How about we stick with Alfred, which we can actually pronounce. What's the deal? Why did Lucifer leave?"

Chris cleared his throat. "Because he trusted his only son to handle things."

Both Isobel and the green dude stared at him.

"Are you saying I'm not capable?"

Holding in a sigh, Isobel poked at his pride. "You have no training. No experience."

"And?"

"Listen to that voice inside. What's it saying?"

Given that his lips flattened, he apparently didn't like what his subconscious told him. "Experience isn't what matters. This is my destiny."

"How about we make sure that destiny lasts more than five minutes?" Her gaze narrowed onto the servant. "Why did his father resign?"

"A servant shouldn't speak of his master to others."

"Except *he* is your master now." She jabbed a finger at Chris. "And I am his wife, which means, if I ask you something, you'd damned well better answer. Right?" She swung her annoyed gaze to Chris, who managed to mutter, "Better listen to her."

"Damned straight, you'd better." She glared at Alfred.

"My apologies, my lady. My lack of respect is intolerable."

"Apologize later. Now, tell me why Lucifer abdicated."

Alfred tucked his hands behind his back. "Rumor has it his new wife is demanding."

"A demanding wife is the best reason to have a high-powered job. To escape her. There's got to be something else," Isobel mulled.

"I know he was dreading the upcoming renovation of the main level of the castle," the butler offered.

"That's grounds for a vacation, not outright quitting."

"There are rumbles of discontent and a possible strike by the Styx boatmen," Alfred stated. "Something about bringing their wages in line with those of the Styx monsters. Which is ludicrous. The monsters work much harder than those lazy oarsmen. All that trying to tip the boats, eating the damned, unable to digest them since their souls won't dissolve. Those monsters earn every penny."

Isobel shook her head. "No, there's got to be something bigger at stake here. Something scary enough he didn't want to stick around."

Her husband finally decided to join the conversation. "He might have said something about the end of the world when he gave me the crown."

"What? And you're just telling me that now?" she screeched.

Chris shrugged. "Because I didn't take it seriously. Keep in mind, I once heard him declare the end of times were coming because Hellflix didn't renew one of his favorite shows."

Except, now, it all made sense. "That dick!" Isobel exclaimed. "Leaving when the going is about to get tough." Or did Lucifer assume that once he left Chris in charge, everything would fall apart?

"Or maybe he was just tired. Dad is old, after all."

"And things are busier than usual," observed Alfred.

"Busier how?" Chris asked.

"It'd be easier to show you, my lord. If you'll follow me, I can take you to your office."

By office, Alfred meant a cavernous room with dragon-melted stone slabs on the floor, soaring ceilings, and a desk made of the skull of some massive, long-dead creature—hopefully extinct. Anything with teeth that large would eat a lot of meat.

Chris entered and took a moment to stare. She couldn't blame him. He'd just reached the next phase of his destiny.

Things were happening now, their lives caught in a snowball rolling down the hill of fate that would end...where?

He circled around the desk to the massive leather chair, the skin of it supple. Chris placed his palms on the surface. "I can't believe this is really happening. I'm going to rule Hell. This is where I'm going to finally make all the decisions."

Alfred cleared his throat. "This is my lord's private office. Nearby is the operations chamber for organizing battles. There is also a throne room where you'll receive supplicants, a high court for those requiring a trial, and then there are the public appearances."

"In other words, I'll be busy."

"Very, my lord."

"This is cause for celebration. We should go out for

dinner," Chris announced, his expression bright and eager. "What do you say, duckie? Should we hit that French place you like?"

Mmm. She did so love fine dining. "It's a date, my king," she said with a wink.

Alfred cleared his throat again, clearly in need of some lozenges. "Leave, my lord? You can't leave."

"I need to eat, Alfred."

"Then food will be brought to you."

"I am not working and eating at the same time. Besides, who says I want Hell food? I'm in the mood for something cooked by a guy with a snooty accent, made in a place that doesn't have ash coating everything."

"Unfortunately, sir, returning to the mortal plane at this time is not possible. Given the extreme influx of souls, we are working at full capacity. Your services are required."

"To do what?"

"Pass judgment, of course. Every soul must receive their due process, and while staff can handle some of the smaller cases, only Hell's King can sign off on each of the case files."

Isobel almost flinched as the other shoe began to drop.

"Paperwork?" Chris lost his happy face. "I'm the king, though."

"Indeed, you are, and as I said, you arrived at a most busy time. The horsemen have been active on the mortal plane. Thousands upon thousands of souls have been arriving of late."

"Then I should be out there, telling the horsemen to stop." Chris went to rise; yet somehow, Alfred— short little fellow that he was—managed to put a hand on his shoulder and shove him back down.

"You will have to let others deal with the horsemen. Your task is here."

Alfred opened a desk drawer and pulled out a sheaf of papers, which he planted on the desk.

"These are the pending files for the souls received this morning." Alfred bent over, and a moment later...

Thud. Another stack hit the desk. "And these are since lunch. Also, there will be a need for a few proclamations."

"What will those be for?" Isobel asked as Chris stared at the growing stack of files.

"Given Hell is under new management, we will, of course, have those who will test the new regime. A speech threatening torture and other things if the populace doesn't cooperate will hopefully suffice to quell any unrest. If not, we can always call out the legions to subdue them."

"Kill people?"

"Kill?" Alfred exclaimed with surprise. "My lord is obviously new. We are in Hell. The damned ones are already dead and cannot be truly killed again. Although, if you feel a need to murder something, you could decimate some of the demons. They do reproduce quickly."

Isobel could see Chris shrinking and jumped in. "Surely some of these tasks can be handed off?"

"Some, yes. However, we are entering a period of great crowding. The more souls that enter, the less room we shall have for everyone. Tempers will flare more than usual. You should prepare a riveting speech to tell the damned they should recycle their souls in the Pit for the good of all. We'll need to increase those numbers drastically if we're going to make room for the new arrivals."

"I hate giving speeches." Chris slumped farther in his chair.

Her poor husband. He'd finally achieved one of his goals. He'd become the King of Fierce Countenance. But, apparently, no one had warned that the expression would be because he was miserable.

And the problem with being married to an unhappy king? It was contagious.

Their new reality set in. Nothing like they'd imagined.

Three days now since they'd been taken prisoner in Hell. At least that was how it felt.

Isobel had once thought how grand it would be to rule over an entire demesne. Now, caught in the bureaucratic nightmare, she wanted out. Especially since the news coming in from topside didn't sound good.

The horsemen had been keeping busy since the dinner party. Pestilence went on a rampage, seeding disease around the world. People even caught her on video, not knowing who it was, wearing a bilious green mini dress, shaking her ass in the clubs. Grinding against people. Touching everything she could. Sowing a deadly plague.

Death—who rumor had it was dating Pestilence—was felling those affected left and right. The hellvine also whispered that he'd claimed some of the plague survivors because they'd touched his girl.

Of course, not everyone knew the horsemen were to blame. Humans assumed someone had launched a biological agent. They began fighting amongst each other, incited by the horseman of war. It didn't take much to convince some leaders and countries to attack each other. Famine joined the game and sucked the life from the fields and the cattle. Food shortages began happening all over. Greed and selfishness turned everyone into paranoid hoarders who stockpiled as much as they could and then defended it to their last dying breath.

Earth was a fucking mess. Chris's words. And they were stuck down below. Like, literally, because he had no idea how to create a portal and no one would create one for him no matter how much he ordered.

Poor Chris. Apparently, respect wasn't automatic with the crown, and he'd yet to learn how to properly instill fear to ensure that they gave it.

"I hate being king," he muttered for the zillionth time that morning from behind the desk with its staggering stacks of files.

"If you hate it so much, then do something to change it."

The words didn't come from Isobel, who sat in a chair, stroking Goshen's massive head, but rather his sister, Muriel, who strode into the office looking rested and vibrant in red jeggings, a slim-fitting tank top, and the cutest little running shoes.

Unlike poor Chris, whose hair stood up in ragged spikes, whose beard needed a comb, and with bags under his eyes large enough to carry groceries.

"What are you doing here?" he snapped. "Come to whine that Daddy didn't leave the kingdom to you?"

Muriel visibly shuddered. "Like fuck. I had a taste of running Hell when Daddy suffered from his bout with goodness." A dark time for everyone because a good Lucifer was worse than an evil one. "I vowed never again."

"You could have warned me," he grumbled as another stack of files dropped out of a portal that suddenly opened overhead. They hit a teetering pile already there and fell over, joining even more damned cases on the floor.

"Would you have listened?" Muriel asked, flinging herself into a seat.

"No." Chris could at least admit the truth. "I thought running Hell was supposed to be cool. Bad-ass.

The only bad thing about it is the sludge they call coffee in this place. No one told me just how much freaking work is involved."

"It is a ton. And with the coming apocalypse, it's going to get worse, which is why Daddy bailed."

"Is there anything we can do to make it stop?" Isobel asked.

"How about I just quit?" Chris grumbled.

Muriel laughed. "You can't quit. Once you're chosen, the job can only be passed on to a willing recipient."

"Fine, then I'll find someone who wants the job."

His sister shook her head. "If only it were that simple. Oh, brother, you have a lot to learn. No one wants to be the Lord of Sin. No one sane, at any rate. And would you really give this chore to someone who would truly torture everyone that comes here?"

"Some deserve it."

At this, Isobel interjected. "Those who've truly sinned and caused harm should be tortured for eternity, but what of the lesser sins? Would you have Hell return to the days of constant brimstone and suffering before Lucifer created the degrees of punishment?" A degree of one was the smallest of sins, barely a slap on the wrist. Get in the triple and quadruple digits, and you were doing hard time. Once your crimes hit seven digits, like the Hitlers and other despots of the world, their suffering was for an eternity.

"I don't want that; however, this has to stop." Chris

slammed his hand on the desk, toppling more of his stacks. "This isn't my destiny."

"You are the Antichrist. Destined to rule Hell. So, yeah, it kind of is." Muriel shrugged. "Sorry. Have you talked to Nef about it?"

Nefertiti, once a powerful sorceress, now resided in Hell as the king's mightiest magic user and adviser.

"The witch?" He frowned. "I met with her only once since my arrival."

Once was enough. Isobel didn't like the way the sultry sorceress eyeballed him and then asked Isobel how much stamina he had in bed. She'd heard stories of Nefertiti's harem and sexploits. The sorceress relied on orgies to fuel her magic, and Isobel wasn't loaning out her husband to give Nefertiti a boost.

Isobel frowned. "What can Nefertiti do to help?"

"She might be able to see a path out of this. A way to either bring Daddy back or find a decent replacement."

"Doesn't the heir need to be related to us?" Chris asked.

A crease marred Muriel's brow. "I don't know. This is the first time the reins of Hell have changed hands. There is no precedent for what we're going through."

"Why are you being so nice?" Chris's brow furrowed, suspicion narrowing his gaze.

"You're my brother from another mother, and while we haven't spent much time together because

I've kind of been going through some stuff, you are family."

The words hit Chris, hit him in the soft spot of his heart that Hell hadn't yet hardened. Still, he scowled. "So this is a pity visit?"

"Nope. Just a 'hey, how's it going?' Things are finally hitting an even keel for me now, which means it's past time we got to know each other."

"I don't want a sister." Said with not much conviction.

"Christopher!" Isobel exclaimed. "That's not nice." The dog, sensing her agitation growled.

A glare was aimed at Goshen, and then Chris shot her a look. "It's true, though. I was happy as an only child."

"Well, I always wanted a brother. So there." Muriel stuck out her tongue, and for a moment, Chris was taken aback.

Then he gave a rueful shake of his head. "I wish you wouldn't do that. I'm supposed to hate you."

"I hate Eva just as much as I love her," Isobel interjected. Her older sister did love to play pranks.

"Don't you dare use the L word, not in here." Muriel peeked around the massive office. "I'm pretty sure Daddy set traps in case anyone ever used it."

"This place is full of secrets," Chris grumbled.

Secrets and locked doors. Isobel had gone exploring a few times—because, unlike Chris, she could escape the paperwork monotony—and had come across sections in the castle that no amount of prying would open. Even Chris, when he took a rare break, couldn't get those doors to open—which only added to his frustration.

"I'd say it was nice to see you, but"—Chris waved a hand—"as you can see, I'm a tad busy."

"No kidding. I'll leave you alone, but I wanted to remind you of Lucinda's upcoming birthday party. You haven't replied to the RSVP."

He grimaced. "I don't do clowns and balloons."

"Neither do I. Horrid things. Daddy saves those for the pedophiles. Ours will be a barbecue—steak, corn on the cob, potato salad. My men love grilling meat. Say you'll come."

"I can't," he grumbled.

Isobel hastened to explain. "It's not that he doesn't want to." Lie. "But more that we can't. He doesn't know how to create a portal to Earth."

Muriel blinked. "But he has magic."

"Erratic magic. It doesn't always do what I want," Chris admitted.

Muriel cocked her head. "How interesting. And if that's the only problem... What if I opened one for you?"

Before Chris could open his mouth and tell her to fuck off, he wasn't attending the party, Isobel jumped in. "That would be lovely. Thank you."

"Awesome. See you around four-ish on Saturday."

Chris waited until Muriel left to snap. "Why the fuck did you say yes? You know I don't want to go."

"Duh," she said with a roll of her eyes. "But didn't you hear what she said? She's going to open a portal to her house. On Earth. Which means a way out of here."

"Out..." His gaze brightened then darkened. "Alfred and the other advisors said I'm not allowed to leave."

At that, she scoffed. "You're the King of Hell. They don't get to give you orders. They work for you."

"They do, don't they?" He drummed his fingers on the desktop. "Surely, they can manage things for a few days while we check out what's happening topside."

Days. Weeks. Months.

Isobel wasn't in a rush to return to Hell. The problem was, the new king didn't want to come back either.

19

Being Hell's King didn't get any easier as the days passed. On the contrary, Chris could feel himself snapping. Even eyed the abyss a time or two. At least in there, he'd find peace and quiet.

Sensing his turmoil, Isobel kept urging him to, "Hold on 'til Saturday."

She clung to hope, whereas he figured his sister had yanked his leg when she said she'd make him a portal to attend the birthday Earth-side. He didn't expect her to keep her word. She'd probably only invited him to be polite.

Yet, there she was, a minute past four in the afternoon, striding into his office, smiling brightly and even giving him a hug, saying, "Glad you're coming, brother. I can't wait for you to meet Lucinda."

Whereas he couldn't wait to escape his Hell prison. He didn't pack anything lest Alfred notice and try to stop them from going. He'd sent the little butler on an errand on the opposite side of the castle.

"We shouldn't make my dear niece wait," Chris said. "Portal away."

"Not here." His sister laughed. "The castle doesn't allow anyone but Daddy to slip in and out."

Did she mean it as a dig? Implying that he couldn't fill their father's shoes? That he was nowhere near as strong? Nowhere near as capable?

Isobel pinched him and hissed, "You've got that look on your face again."

The one that betrayed that he was in over his head with no clue what the fuck to do.

Lucifer had eons to hone this machine, to practice and rule over Hell. Chris didn't even get an instruction manual, and the longer he remained in the Pit, the less he knew. The more he felt his sanity slipping.

It didn't help that he'd tried to call for his mother, caving to the need for help, only to have her ignore his call.

Nothing worse than standing in front of a mirror and saying, "Mother? Mommy? Mum. Fucking cunt that birthed me," and not having a single whisper back.

Abandoned. Again. But this time, the stakes were much higher.

"Why don't you show us where you can portal us out?" Isobel said.

"We just need to get outside the castle walls." Muriel spun and left the office.

Isobel's fingers wrapped tightly around his as they followed his sister through the courtyard, Goshen trailing at their heels. They were only halfway across when he heard the dreaded cry.

"My lord. Stop."

"Run!" He gave Isobel a shove. "Save yourself." Alfred had caught them. So much for an easy escape.

"I'm not going without you." His staunchest ally planted herself by his side.

Dammit. She could have left and maybe found a way to come back for him.

But, no, she just had to love him too much. Chris sighed as he whirled around, only to blink as Muriel screamed. "Polkie!"

His sister then broke into a very un-princess-like run. She grabbed hold of Alfred and swung him around. The top of his bald, spotted head turned an interesting shade of purple.

"Mistress Satana. Delightful to see you," Alfred sputtered.

"And you," she exclaimed. "You're looking fit. Chris must be keeping you busy." She glanced over her shoulder. "Polkie is happiest when he's got lots of work to do. I used to do my best to make sure he had plenty."

"No one has ever managed to match your antics. You truly had a gift for pranks." Said with a fond smile, which, for the uninitiated, had too many pointed teeth.

"I don't suppose I can tear you away from the castle to come to a party. It's for Lucinda. And before you say it, I know she's not even technically a year old, but given Lilith made her grow up too fast, we thought it only right that we try and give her some of the things she missed."

"I wish I could, mistress. However, my workload is much too great." Alfred's gaze swung toward Chris. The king pretended interest in the ashy skyline, which he still didn't understand. There was no actual sun, and yet Hell did lighten and darken, keeping a pattern of day and night.

Night being a time not recommended for the less violent souls in the Pit. Being somewhat fleshy and edible, he and Isobel didn't venture forth from their rooms during that time.

Muriel kissed Alfred's head. "One of these days, Polkie, I'm going to drag you out for a few hours of nothing but fun."

His face wrinkled. "I do wish you wouldn't. There are those waiting for me to lapse so they might steal my prestigious spot."

"If anyone dares, I'll skewer them myself," she said. "I wish I could stay and chat, but I've got to get back to Lucinda. I left Bambi in charge of dressing her, which means Auric will probably blow a gasket. He has no sense of style."

"We can't have your consort hurting himself. Not now with the end of times coming," Alfred announced.

"The end of times had better wait until after the cake." Muriel scowled. "Lucinda will have a meltdown if someone ruins it. We'd better get moving." Said to Chris.

Alfred noticed and cleared his throat. "Um, my lord."

Before his servant could start lecturing him again about his duties, Chris barked, "I'm going, Alfred, and that's final."

"Of course, you must, my lord. She is your niece. But you forgot the gift." Alfred held out his webbed hand. In it was a tiny box.

Isobel was the one to reach out and snatch it. "Thanks, er, Polkie?" she replied on a querying note, testing out the name. "See ya later."

They continued on their way, out the gate where Muriel sketched a portal. Chris kept expecting someone to tell him he couldn't go. But no one stopped them, and a moment later, they were back on Earth.

Sweet fucking Earth. Chris hit the ground and pressed his lips to it, murmuring, "I missed you."

Freaky thing was, he got a reply.

"Missed you too, my son. See you soon."

Shit.

20

PUTTING the finishing touches on her niece's makeup, Bambi stepped back and smiled. "Don't you look darling, lambkin."

"She looks like she's ready to go clubbing," grumbled Auric as he entered his daughter's room—also nicknamed the pink monstrosity. "You do realize she's a child."

"And?" Perusing Lucinda's face, Bambi couldn't see what his problem was. "I used pink for her lips and, look, mascara this time instead of fake lashes."

"Did it ever occur to you to just put her hair in braids and not put any makeup on her at all?"

At his complaint, Lucinda giggled. "Oh, Daddy. You're silly. Don't I look pretty?"

At the dulcet, lisped query, his face softened. "You are always beautiful, baby girl." He held out his arms, and she hopped into them. "Are you ready for your party?"

"Un-huh." She nodded her head. "I wanna dance. Auntie Bambi says she's gonna teach me to twerk."

He glared over her head. "Auntie Bambi is going to keep her moves to rated G, as in good for all audiences."

"Such a spoilsport." But Bambi laughed. While she did love to tease Auric, she would never do anything to ruin her niece's innocence. No one dared, not when they all knew the power potential encased in her little body. The sweeter and kinder they taught her to be, the better it would be for everyone in the long run.

She followed Auric as he carried his daughter downstairs, patiently answering her thousand and one questions.

"Did Mommy make a cake?"

Less make, more like catered. "She did."

"And we have ba-woons?" Said with an adorable accent.

"Yes, David got you balloons."

"And a tent for Uncle T?"

"The tent is up." A thick canvas affair that meant Teivel, Muriel's vampire mate, could also be present for the barbecue.

"Wait until you see the piñata David bought." Auric snickered, and with good reason. They'd commissioned a plaster of Ursula that they'd all get to whack with a stick.

"Tristan"—Muriel's merman consort, because her sister had four, yes *four* men to satisfy her—"made sure the pool is nice and warm. Wait until you show Daddy your new swimsuit." Bambi winked, and Lucinda giggled when Auric growled.

Overprotective daddies were so awesome. Not something Bambi knew firsthand, but she did so enjoy her clients who liked to role-play.

"Mommy says Uncle Christopher is coming, too."

"Because Mommy is nuts," Auric mumbled. He wasn't crazy about the Antichrist being invited to his daughter's party, especially with all the shit happening in the world.

An army of the dead gathered on the mortal plane. One led by Christopher's mother. To what purpose, no one yet knew. But at least she'd finally called back her horsemen to act as generals for her troops.

However, the fact that she no longer sowed death and discord didn't reassure. What did she plan to do with all those dead soldiers? Where were they? Because, somehow, Morgana had managed to hide them with her magic.

And why did Bambi have a knot in her gut? Must have been the cock she'd gobbled for breakfast. Curried semen that early in the morning always gave her indigestion.

As they hit the bottom steps, the doorbell rang.

"Can you grab that?" Auric asked. "I told Muriel

I'd get some pictures of Lucinda in her party dress before she gets messy."

"I don't get messy. Much." Spoken with an adorable dimple.

"Go take some pretty pics. Remember how Auntie showed you to smile."

Lucinda did duck lips, and Auric groaned.

With a laugh, Bambi shooed him off and veered toward the front hall. Despite a coat of paint, she could still see a faint black line where little miss naughty had taken a marker to the walls. Lucinda's picture was in the dictionary under the word *handful*. The teenage years would be interesting.

Upon answering the door, Bambi's mouth rounded into an O of surprise. "Charlie? I didn't know Muriel invited you."

Looking casual in his polo shirt and slacks with his blond hair in artful disarray, Charlie shrugged and offered a rueful smile. "She didn't, but I overheard someone talking about the party, so I thought I'd pop in. We are, after all, family, and I do love cake. I hope it's okay."

"Sure." Although she had to wonder why Charlie suddenly chose now to reach out to the Baphomet side. And look at that, he'd brought a guest. A petite Asian woman, who clung to his arm and ducked her head shyly. "Um, come in." They entered, and Bambi shivered as if someone ran a feather up her spine.

The tiny woman whispered something to Charlie.

"Washroom?" he asked.

Still bemused, Bambi pointed, and the female scurried off with a nod of thanks. Bambi arched a brow at her not-often-seen cousin.

"You crashed a party *and* brought a date? Was that wise?" They couldn't exactly hide the oddity of Muriel's special mates. A fallen angel, a shapeshifter, a vampire, and a merman. Her sister had quite the collection.

"Don't worry," said Charlie. "Lee is cool. I met her in the Himalayas. You can't tell by looking at her, but she's kitsune." A Japanese shapeshifting fox.

"You do know Hell's King might be coming?"

"I thought he retired."

"He did. Lucifer is off somewhere tropical. I was talking about Chris."

"I'm not worried about Chris. He and I are cool."

"Last time I saw you, he was trying to light your ass on fire."

"We've worked things out since." The bright, white smile meant to reassure brought a frown.

"What about your dad?" Elyon wouldn't approve.

"Don't worry about my dad. He's got other stuff to keep him busy."

Probably sorting his white socks by color. Elyon was dull. Bambi never understood how Lucifer tolerated him, and yet when it came to playing chess—or golf—the first person he always invited was his brother.

"The party is out back."

"Go. I'll be along in a second." He inclined his head to the closed washroom door.

Bambi left with a wasted sashay of her hips. While not picky about her lovers, and meals, she never fed on family. Even first cousins. A succubus, even the world's sluttiest one, had to have some lines she wouldn't cross.

Exiting into the yard—which, despite the heavy tent surrounding it, was lit with bright lights and the ceiling painted light blue—she noted everything ready. The patio set looked inviting with its plush cushions. The tables for the food and drinks were covered in pink tablecloths. Balloons festooned everything, helium ones that floated.

They would also provide entertainment later on after a few beers when the boys inhaled the gas and talked in chipmunk voices. She'd charged her phone to make sure she videotaped it.

The outdoor barbecue was a massive brick affair with its own chimney, which meant they wouldn't die of the fumes but they could still smell the charcoal. Yum.

Noticing that Muriel was missing, she said, "Where's lamb?"

Teivel, busy rolling the keg into place, replied, "Went to fetch Chris. Should be back any second now."

She headed back inside and wandered into the kitchen where she found Auric taking pictures.

Lucinda was being a ham. Refusing to smile. Sticking out her tongue.

"Oooh, you brat. You know your mommy wants a nice one."

Lucinda giggled. "Mommy loves my silly face."

She did. Muriel and everyone who met Lucinda loved the little brat.

A hellion who saw more things than she should.

Her niece stopped laughing for a moment and cocked her head. Her face went blank, and her voice took on a spooky cast as she channeled the kid from *Poltergeist* announcing in a singsong voice, "They're here."

21

NOT EVEN HERE TEN seconds and already hearing his mother's voice. The fact that she'd so easily found him froze Chris and heated him at the same time. It also meant a change in strategy.

The original plan that he and Isobel had concocted—one that relied on Muriel actually helping them escape Hell—had them slipping away from the party and going to ground. AKA hiding and traveling the world, free of duty, free of the Pit.

Then Mommy said hello. *I can't leave now.* What if his mother pulled the same shit she had at the dinner party? He may not want a sister or a niece, but that didn't mean he would run away and let them face his mother alone.

Despite the comforting feeling of soil—solid, real, earthy, the scent of decay and everything that fertilized it a balm to his soul—Chris stood and surveyed his surroundings. His surprising surroundings.

"You live in the country?" he exclaimed. They stood in a pasture, stubby grass underfoot, with white fencing all around to keep a pair of horses from fleeing.

Muriel planted her hands on her hips, lifted her face to the sky, and breathed deeply. "Yup. Turns out I'm more a country girl than expected. Which is a practical thing given I have strange visitors at times. Rather than spend all our time hiding in the city and suburbia, we thought it best to stay far away from neighbors."

"Understandable." Yet weird for a guy who'd grown up knowing only the mundane world. He'd never imagined the intricate layers of paranormal hidden from humans. Once concealed from him, as well. Yet, as it turned out, the supernatural was all around him. Only now, he actually noticed it.

Goshen dashed ahead of them, acting almost doglike, his nose to the ground, sniffing. Peeing on the one rock they could see. Chris laced his fingers through Isobel's as they crossed the field to a gate, watching for piles of steaming doo-doo. In the distance, he noted a massive tent abutting a house.

"Getting the place fumigated?" he asked, which seemed odd given the party.

Muriel laughed. "Nope. That's to make sure Teivel doesn't turn into a pile of ash. He and the sun don't get along."

"Then why not have the party at night?"

Muriel shrugged. "Because Lucinda insisted we have it in the afternoon. And when little missy feels that strongly about something, sometimes it's easier to say yes."

"My mother never gave in to my requests," Isobel noted. "She's very bossy."

At that, Muriel chuckled, a low, throaty, contagious sound. "So am I, usually. Which means we have some interesting moments, my daughter and I. In this case, because it was her very first birthday party, I kind of gave in to most of her demands."

"Which ones did you kibosh?" asked Chris.

"I said no to getting a dinosaur for rides, and I wouldn't let her invite her human classmates. I was worried someone would eat them."

There was just no reply to that.

They'd not quite made it to the tent when there was a screech in the air.

Looking up, Chris's eyes widened while Isobel squeaked and hid behind him. He felt an urge to hide too, but since his sister didn't throw herself to the ground and cower, he fought the urge. Still... "I thought you said no dinosaurs?"

"That's a dragon," Muriel announced with a scowl.

"For real? A fucking dragon?" And not just any dragon. A pink one, with wide wings and a long tail. "I didn't know you owned a dragon." Then again, he didn't know they actually existed. This was the first one he'd ever seen.

"She is so grounded," his sister growled in a low tone.

"Who is grounded?"

"Lucinda. She knows her dragon is supposed to stay in Hell at her poppa's stable, but she keeps making portals and sneaking her in."

"Lucinda can make a portal?" Could his shame get any worse? Even a little girl could accomplish what he couldn't.

"Your niece is a bit of a brat, who needs to mind her mother's rules." Muriel scowled.

"She's a kid. I'm sure she'll grow out of it." Hopefully, she would remain powerful, though, because it totally made her a possible contender to take over his wretched reign as King of Hell. "How old is she again?" How long until he could hand over his crown and run for the hills?

"Old enough to know better." It wasn't the reply he'd hoped for.

Reaching the tent, Muriel shouted, "Coming in, duck and hide, Teivel."

She yanked on a flap, the Velcro seams coming apart with a familiar ripping sound. They slipped in, and Chris blinked. It was brighter inside the tent than outside.

He then blinked again as he noticed the man before him. Dark hair, penetrating gaze, and hawkish features. The stranger eyed him up and down.

"You must be the brother," he finally muttered,

looking less than impressed. "I expected someone taller."

In Hell, Chris might have ordered his guards to make the man show some respect. On Earth, he had to do it himself. "That's 'your majesty,' asshole."

"Chris!" Isobel slapped him. "He's joking." Not really, but his wife gushed on. "You must be Teivel. Pleasure. I'm Isobel, and this is my husband, Chris, Hell's King."

"Hmph," Teivel's replied before he walked away.

"Pleasant fellow," Chris muttered.

"I think he prefers the term stoic," Muriel replied. "Don't worry, he'll come around. He was kind of miffed when Daddy gave you the job. He wanted me to have it because he actually likes Hell."

"I'll just bet he does." Chris took a look around, impressed by the fact that the tent managed to cover not only the patio area by the house but also a large in-ground pool.

Lifting a hand, Muriel waved at another guy across on the other side of the tent. "David, come see who came to the party."

"Another lover?" joked a man with long hair held away from his face at his nape.

"Not today. But Polkie says the apocalypse is coming, so you never know," Muriel sang.

Chris found his hand engulfed in a handshake that crushed his bones. He eyed the fellow in front of him, and his nose tickled. "You got a cat around here?"

Because that was the only thing that usually set off his allergies.

Once again, Isobel elbowed him. "Would you stop that?"

"Stop what?" He adopted his most guileless face. Yeah, he was fucking with the dude. He'd read the files on his brothers-in-law. Muriel had quite the collection.

So far, he'd met the vampire, Teivel. In front of him was the shapeshifter, David, which meant the jovial fellow who vaulted from the pool, water sluicing from his very toned body, his swim trunks hanging low on his hips, had to be the merman, Tristan. Chris's fingers itched for a harpoon.

Thankfully, he didn't have to gut the man because Isobel moved away with Muriel and didn't ogle the fellow up close.

"You must be the fish-man," Chris said. Son of Neptune. Some hotshot in the ocean. Thankfully, married.

"The correct term is merman, and you might want to watch the attitude," Tristan said, smiling pleasantly. "Muriel might be giddy at finally getting to know her brother, but we're not as gullible."

"Which is his polite way of saying fuck her or the child over and die." This from the vampire, who flashed some fang.

Usually, Chris would have given some flippant, partially assholish answer. However, he kind of liked his new sister—a little—and given it was a kid's birthday party, he shrugged and said, "It's cool."

Cooler still was the glare he got from the last dude, Muriel's main consort, who emerged from the house, his gaze scanning everything before landing on Chris and staying there. That one look reiterated the vampire's threat.

Fuck with my family and die. Nice welcome.

Still, he was the Antichrist, and he could handle some overprotective dudes. What he wasn't armored against was cuteness.

Flying out of the house, hair in pigtails, her face painted like a miniature beauty queen, was a little girl. She squealed, "Uncle Chris!" and threw herself at him. It seemed rude not to catch her.

"Happy to meetcha," she said, hugging him tighter and, in the process, wrapping him around her tiny little finger.

"Um, ditto," said the suave King of Hell.

"We're gonna have so much fun!" She batted incredibly long lashes as she snuggled him.

"I, uh, have a present." He managed to fumble the small gift out and hand it to the squirming mass in his arms.

"Oooh. Gimme." She tore into the paper and opened the box before he blinked. Inside, an amulet with a vivid pink stone. Not exactly what he would have chosen, but Lucinda beamed.

It went around her neck, and she clasped it in one

pudgy fist. "I wuv it. It's my favorite-est thing evah! Next to you, of course, Uncle Chris."

For some reason, this unnerved him. "I can't stay too long. Things to do. You know."

The biggest eyes rose to meet his. "You can't leave before the cake," she lisped. "Or you'll miss the big surprise."

"What surprise?"

But all he got was a giggle.

"Baby girl, get your cute butt over here so Mommy can get a picture," Muriel yelled, waving her phone.

"But Daddy already took some," Lucinda remarked.

"I want another. Now, young lady."

"Party pooper." The lower lip jutted, and for a moment, red flashed inside the irises of her eyes. Then the smile returned. "Gotta go!" Lucinda bounced out of his arms, and he stared after her. Fascinated. Also slightly afraid because he'd felt the power in her tiny body. So. Much. Power.

Isobel sidled close and whispered, "When are we sneaking away?"

"We're not. Not yet." Because something was going to happen. Lucinda might have implied it, but inside he could feel it. "Let's stay for the cake at least."

"Okay." Isobel gave him an odd look but went with the flow.

Chris didn't quite join the festivities, choosing to

sit under the tent and watch as Muriel had her daughter pose, alone and with each of her daddies.

He'd not heard his mother's voice again but knew he hadn't imagined it. Nor did he mention it to Isobel. Let her enjoy herself. She chatted with Bambi, a glass of wine in hand, looking more relaxed than he'd seen her in days.

As for him, he enjoyed the steady stream of beer coming from the keg. He'd missed amber ale. The stuff in Hell burned going in and even more coming out.

Everything was going great.

Too great.

Too smoothly.

Which meant something would fuck it up. He just hoped it wouldn't be him.

Or his mother.

You hear that, Mommy Dearest? Leave this little girl and her party alone.

But it wasn't Morgana who arrived to ruin the day.

22

Lucifer arrived wearing a loud shirt covered in flamingoes and board shorts that did not cover enough of his hairy legs.

"Grandpa is here!" he exclaimed, flinging his arms wide.

For a moment, everyone stared.

Even Muriel. "Daddy, I didn't think you were coming."

No one did. Last time Bambi had spoken to Lucifer, he'd been quite adamant on that point. Gaia was due to pop at any time. Since Mother Earth's midwife had forbidden any kind of interdimensional travel, she'd grounded Lucifer with her.

The Devil never did do well with rules and ultimatums.

"Fooled you all," he boomed. "As if I'd miss my granddaughter's party. How else am I supposed to give her a gift?" He knelt as Lucinda flew at him. He didn't even flinch at her exuberant and loving hug, probably because the greedy child asked, "What did you bring me?"

"Me? What makes you think I'd spoil a little princess rotten?" He winked, and Lucinda giggled.

"Gimme!" She held out her pudgy hands.

Snapping his fingers, he snatched something out of midair, which he dropped into her cupped hands, a square piece of paper. Bambi squinted but couldn't see what was on it.

An epic squeal emerged from Lucinda.

Muriel winced. "Oh, fuck. What did you give her now?"

It was David, his long, blond hair held back in a ponytail, who peeked over Lucifer's shoulder to declare, "It's a picture of some kind of sea monster."

"A picture?" Muriel repeated doubtfully.

"Of her new pet!" Lucifer declared. "You all remember Sweets." Given there were a few blank looks, Lucifer explained. "Adexios, Charon's kid, has a pet sea monster. The one-eyed, purple beast had a baby. As soon as I saw it, I knew it was just the thing for the most perfect granddaughter ever created."

"I love it!" Lucinda clapped her hands before Muriel could say, "No."

At least, this time, Lucifer didn't hide the gift. It took several singed rooms and a few missing neighborhood pets before Muriel had found out about Lucinda's last pet—the pink dragon.

"Mommy, isn't she boo-tiful," Lucinda lisped, batting her lashes—just like Auntie taught her. Bambi couldn't help but swell with pride.

"We don't have room for it," Muriel began to explain, only to have Tristan clear his throat. "Um, actually, we kind of do. Remember how I had some surveys done of the land. Turns out, the house is sitting above an underground cavern with a massive lake, which not only means we'd have room for it, but it would be hidden, too."

Muriel groaned. "Why me?"

To which her husbands, all four of them, laughed and said, "Because you're Lucifer's daughter."

Which seemed to be explanation enough.

Of course, with that many Baphomets gathered in one spot, it wasn't hard to predict that things would happen. Things always did around those who were special. And Bambi didn't mean the kind of special that licked the pavement and growled at the neighbors.

Lucifer's family drew attention. Usually from the cops, who got calls of weird shit happening, but it also drew the attention of cryptids and supernaturals.

As the music played—Justin Bieber hits because Lucinda had a crush—and the beer flowed—because it took alcohol to tolerate family parties—Bambi noticed one guest who'd yet to make an appearance in the yard.

Where had Charlie and his date gone?

The moment she entered the house, the knot in her stomach got bigger. Especially when she saw him at the front door with his little Asian companion. A door that was wide-open so he could greet the people coming in.

Allowing Isobel's mother to enter along with Rasputin was fine, but those following?

What had Charlie done? Bambi opened her mouth to yell a warning.

Only she never managed to give it. A hand slapped over her mouth, a strong one covered in a rusty red glove. The aroma of a man who lived in his armor surrounded her, musky and enticing, almost as sexy as the gravelly voice against her ear that said, "Make not a sound, my lady. I would hate to bind your sweet flesh."

With such a tempting offer, Bambi shoved against War, then turned on him with a bright gaze—hard nipples and a wet pussy—and hollered, "We have party crashers." Then she held out her wrists and said, "Cuff me, hot stuff."

23

CHRIS COULD HAVE SWORN he'd heard his sister yell something about visitors.

The more, the merrier.

With a warm buzz flowing through him, he even managed a smile when his old buddy War—who had tried to kill him and failed back in the good ol' days— stepped into the tent, Bambi clinging to his arm.

"War! Dude. Long time no see." He waved; however, everyone else kind of stopped what they were doing to stare. Understandable. War thrived on violence. But Chris was happy to see him anyway. Blame the beer for making him nostalgic.

However, not everyone seemed happy that War had decided to crash the party. Bodies moved. Lucinda was shuffled behind two of her daddies. Muriel drew a cool, flaming sword. David was no longer David, but a giant kitty, and Teivel suddenly looked a lot bigger and menacing. And did those fangs in his mouth get longer?

As for Lucifer? He jabbed a finger in War's direction, and said, "You! Thanks for all your murderous efforts lately. Finally gave me the push I needed to retire."

Which reminded Chris... "You." He jabbed his own finger. "Would you stop it with the battles and killing already? You're burying me in paperwork."

War didn't reply, simply stiffened as he stepped aside, allowing Isobel's mother and grandfather to enter. Followed by—

"Daddy!" Isobel screamed as she launched herself at the distinguished gent accompanying them.

Daddy? What the fuck was happening? Last time Chris had seen Thomas, he'd been a motionless corpse on an altar, his spirit holding the remaining seal on Morgana's prison shut. Since the slab was empty, and his mother had escaped, Chris had assumed the man dead. Yet here he was, looking rather hale and hearty.

As Isobel's family poured into the tent, the other horsemen arrived. Pestilence appeared especially festive in her yellow hazmat suit. Death had on a fresh cowl, and Famine looked rather well fed in his white suit and brown loafers with no socks.

Not exactly the kind of guests you wanted to see at a kid's birthday. No wonder Muriel and her hubbies appeared pissed.

It was Isobel's dad who held up his hands when

Muriel stalked close and aimed her sword. "Everyone hold off before attacking. This isn't what you think."

Muriel refused to put away her sword. "You're crashing my kid's party."

"We're here to help," said Chris's father-in-law, spreading his hands in a gesture of peace.

"Help by bringing the horsemen of the apocalypse?" Isobel backed away until she stood by Chris's side, a crease between her brows. "I don't understand, Papa. Where have you been? Why are you here? And why are you here with *them*?"

Nefertiti, who arrived at that moment, carrying a Jell-O ring, was the one to answer. "It's the day of the apocalypse. And everyone's invited."

"Today! Are you fucking kidding me?" Muriel snapped, turning her head too many degrees to bark at the witch. "One afternoon. That's all I freaking wanted. One afternoon to celebrate my darling little girl."

"Did you really expect her to have a mundane party? As stupid as your mother." This spoken by the one person capable of making Chris groan.

"Who is that?" Muriel yelled.

"My mother," said Chris with a sigh. So much for getting out of the castle and relaxing.

At the sign of the first tear in the side of the tent, and daylight spilling in, Muriel screamed. "Teivel, get out of here. Take Lucinda with you. Get yourselves to the vault."

Her fanged hubby scooped up the little girl, who pouted. "But I want to stay and watch!"

To which Muriel snarled, "You will go with him. Now, young lady."

"You're no fun. I hate you," squealed her daughter, still looking cute.

Muriel hollered at Auric. "Do something about your kid."

"Little busy right now," he claimed, sword in hand, facing the bulging walls.

"Great, make me be the bad parent again. Go. Now. Or there will be no cake!" Muriel ordered, pointing her sword toward the house.

With her lower lip still jutting, Lucinda left with Teivel, escaping to the relative safety of the house. Which was better than being out in the yard with the bulging walls of the tent.

When Chris spotted the first decayed hand poking through the canvas, he knew Mother hadn't crashed the party alone.

"Mother!" he bellowed. "You weren't invited."

As if speaking to her was the sign she'd awaited, the side of the tent ripped open large enough for Morgana to saunter in, an army of the dead at her back.

Mother stopped and surveyed them, hands empty, but then again, who needed a weapon when you could call magic? She looked rather lovely, too, dressed in battle armor, but a kind made for a lady.

Her red gown was overlain with a thick metal

corset, her arms encased in onyx metal guards. She even wore a helmet with a nose guard, which drew attention to the bottomless pits of her eyes.

Muriel stood facing her, flaming sword in hand.

"At last, we meet. I've heard a lot about you," Muriel said.

His mother looked down her nose at his sister. "If it isn't the other bastard child."

"Actually," Lucifer interjected, clearing his throat, "I did marry her mother. Damnable woman made an honest man of me."

"What a shame she'll soon be a widow." Morgana's gaze brooked no quarter.

"You are not murdering my daughter's poppa on her birthday," Muriel declared.

"Don't you mean, ever, Muri?" Lucifer added.

"My quarrel isn't with you, Daughter of the Earth. But I will have my vengeance against he who locked me away. But not today. Today, I am here for my son."

"What now?" Chris groaned. "I told you I wanted nothing to do with you. Especially not after the stunt you pulled with Isobel. You almost killed her."

"Almost. Since she is here alive and well, I obviously failed in my last attempt."

"And it won't happen again," Thomas interjected. "We've had a talk, Morgana and I."

"You've been talking to my mother-in-law?" Isobel rolled her eyes. "Seriously? And yet you couldn't call me to say, 'hey, baby girl, still alive.'"

"My fault." Marya joined the conversation. "I was the one to release him from the crypt and then hid him until I could make him understand the true plan."

"You mean you knew he was alive all this time?" A note of betrayal tinged her words. Isobel turned to her grandfather. "Did you know, too?"

Rasputin shrugged. "Yes. But I wasn't aware Marya had released him. Last Christopher and I saw Thomas, he was still in the crypt."

Oh, shit. Way to drag him into the mess. Eyes full of betrayal turned on him. "You knew, too! You lied to me!" Eyes flashing, Isobel stomped off.

He reached for her. "Let me explain."

She slapped away his hand. "Don't touch me right now. I need some space. And a bathroom." Isobel left, and Lucifer chuckled.

"This party is even more interesting than I expected. Totally wishing I had a bucket of popcorn right about now."

"Stuff it, you old goat. No one is interested in listening to you right now," Chris snapped.

"Finally, my son comes to his senses," Morgana crowed.

"You can shut it, too. I want to know why you're here," Chris demanded. Anything to stall having to chase his wife and grovel for forgiveness.

"Where else would I be?" Morgan tilted her head. "The battle is about to start."

"I thought you said you weren't here to fight," Muriel stated.

"I am not here to fight you, or even your lecherous father. I'm here to support my son. To keep him on Hell's throne."

"Then who are you planning to fight? Because none of us want to take his spot," Muriel replied, still not sheathing her sword.

"Isn't it obvious? I'm here to fight God and his heavenly host."

Before anyone could laugh, the tent collapsed.

24

Isobel fled the party, escaped the people who'd betrayed her.

She brushed off her father, who said he wanted to explain. Explain what? How he'd let her believe he was dead?

She ignored her mother because she'd obviously known her dad was alive.

As for Grandfather, the last peek over her shoulder showed him sidling up to the Devil. Probably trying to find out if his previous deal for prime real estate on the Styx was still good.

Even Chris had let her down. *He knew. I can't believe he knew and lied to me.*

The coolness of the air conditioning hit Isobel's fevered skin the moment she entered the house, and once she slammed the door shut, the quiet surrounded her, as well. She needed a moment to herself to try and figure out what had happened and whom she should be mad at.

Everyone was on her shit list at the moment. Which meant she should take a step back, remove emotions from the equation, and look at why, why, and why?

Why was Daddy here? Why now? And what had Nefertiti meant when she said it was the day of the apocalypse? She'd brought dessert. Did that mean she expected it to happen later?

Did Isobel have time for a last-minute quickie with Chris?

Wait, I'm supposed to be mad at him. It bothered her that he'd hidden the truth about her dad from her. Then again, he seemed to think her dad wouldn't be coming back. He didn't fake the surprise when Papa appeared.

From inside the house, she heard Lucinda complaining. "I wanna go back outside. It's my party!"

A low rumbled reply of, "Mommy said to stay inside where it's safe," resulted in a foot stomp that made the house tremble.

That little girl was going to be a handful. Would a child of hers and Chris's also have too much power? How would they raise a kid without letting the power go to his or her head?

She just had to recall Chris and his arrogance when they'd first met to know that they'd have their work cut out for them. *If* they had kids.

The apocalypse was coming. She'd better pee while she had a chance. She'd been peeing a lot more the past few days. Must be Hell and all that dry heat. She'd probably been retaining more water than usual to combat it.

Washing her hands, feeling a little more relaxed, she emerged and squeaked as she came face-to-face with Charlie.

"Goodness," she exclaimed, pressing a hand to her racing heart. "You scared me. I didn't know you were here."

"I was waiting for the right moment."

"Moment for what?" she asked. "They were just about to slap the steaks on when I left." And possibly get into a great big old brawl, given her daddy had brought the horsemen of the apocalypse.

"I didn't come for the food. I came for you."

She blinked at him. "Excuse me?"

"I love you, Isobel. I want you to come away with me. Now, before it's too late."

"What do you mean 'too late?' Don't tell me you think the world is going to end today, too?"

Why wasn't it on anyone's calendar? She might have worn a different outfit if she'd known.

"The world is going to end. As is your husband's short reign."

"You are not killing my husband."

"I'm not, although I will be taking his spot. Father says leading Hell is the perfect job for me, given my attitude. Sell a few weapons to infidels, and Dad says I'm breaking his rules," Charlie complained.

"You can't become King of Hell. The mantle can only go to a descendent of Lucifer's." That much was made clear when she and Chris had explored possibilities.

"I know all about the genetics behind ruling the Pit. Which is why you and I will marry. And I will be the regent."

She blinked at his logic. "Marrying me if Chris is dead won't mean you inherit."

"I won't through you, but the child in your belly will."

Belly? She stared down, and her eyes widened in horror. "I'm pregnant!"

"Yes, which initially wasn't my ideal scenario, but as Father pointed out, I need the child to become regent. So, it will all work out."

"Except I want nothing to do with your plan. I don't love you."

"You will. I'm Jesus. Everyone loves me." He gave his most engaging smile, but it lacked the leering of her husband's. He also only had golden good looks rather than the dark and sexy appeal of her Antichrist lover.

Isobel angled her chin. "You need to leave. Now. Before I call for help."

"I'm leaving, but not alone. You're coming with me." He grabbed hold of her.

"I'm not going anywhere with you." She yanked her arm, which he held in a tight grip.

"Oh, yes you are. I can't have you accidentally dying in the coming battle."

"What battle?"

"The one between Heaven and Hell. Dad is going to be here any minute. I sent Lee back to Heaven with directions to the house. Did you know Lucifer had it hidden from Dad's angels? I had to bring one here in person in order to forge a trail."

"A trail for who? What did you do?" she asked.

"Just let Daddy know where the party was. Can you believe he wasn't invited? Neither was I, for that matter. Rude, if you ask me. Good thing Chris let me know about it."

"Wait, what? What does Chris have to do with it?"

"I told him we needed to trap his mother. The plan was he'd lure her here, and I'd let Dad know so he could handle Morgana."

"What's your dad going to do?" Pontificate? She'd heard Elyon was good at that.

"He's going to cleanse the world of sin, starting with Morgana and her army of the dead."

"But I thought Elyon didn't care what happened on Earth."

"Used to be he didn't pay it much attention; however, he recently subscribed to a few social media channels and started watching current events. Noticed the rise of sin. How evil has spread everywhere. He's decided it's time to cleanse the world. To conduct another purge."

Her eyes widened. "He's going to cause another flood!"

Charlie's nose wrinkled. "Nope. Last time, some of the clever folks built an ark and escaped his punishment, which is why he has a better plan this time."

Before she could ask about what that was, there came a series of knocks at the door.

"Look who's here," Charlie said as he opened the front door, revealing his fatherly deity in all his bearded glory. "Time for phase two of our plan."

"A wondrous day for all mankind," Elyon declared from the front stoop. "It is time, as the humans say, to cut the head off the snake."

She had a feeling she knew who he thought the snake was. "Don't you dare hurt my husband." Or anyone else, for that matter.

But Elyon didn't even acknowledge her words. Although he did cough something that sounded suspiciously like, "unclean whore."

"I am married!" she retorted hotly as Charlie dragged her out the door, past his dad. She turned back to see God striding into Muriel's house, a host of angels at his back, their wings tucked in tightly, their swords dangling by their sides. As shadows danced around her from overhead, she glanced up to see a flock of angels—hundreds, thousands maybe—filling the skies. Unbeknownst to those in the tent.

"You're going to let him massacre everyone," she exclaimed.

"It's the only way to eradicate sin. Don't worry. You'll be safe."

But she didn't want to be safe. She wanted her husband. Only Charlie wouldn't let her go. And her magic wasn't responding. Which meant she got stuffed into a chariot drawn by four white, winged horses.

Only once they were aloft did she notice the second army gathered below, the stain of their dead bodies a blight on the land.

And Chris was caught between them.

25

THE TENT COLLAPSED, but with so many magic users gathered in one place, instead of being buried under yards of tarp, the fabric turned into ash, which meant that Chris could clearly see they were totally fucked.

On the ground, all around, was an army of the dead. Overhead, angels with swords.

And they were pinched between them.

Only... "Um, is it me," Muriel asked, "or are we being protected by the horsemen of the apocalypse?"

Sure enough, War and his buddies formed a circle around Chris, Muriel, and his mom. His dad was also in there, but more by accident than design he'd wager.

Outside that ring, three of Muriel's hubbies fought; only the dead weren't hitting them back.

"What's happening?" Chris asked as the flock of angels dove upon the zombies with fluting cries of triumph.

"This is an attack on your reign. God wants you dead," his mother announced, raising her hand and deflecting a white-winged angel with a blue blast of light that sent it tumbling away.

"Me?" He couldn't help a note of astonishment. "What the fuck did I ever do to him?"

"You exist," was her reply.

"I'm a little offended," Lucifer interjected. "I've been pissing my brother off for eons. Yet put my son in charge for a few days, and Elyon goes to war? Unfair, I say."

"Die, unholy demon!" An angel with a massive wingspan dove at them, eyes alight with righteousness, the sword in his hand slightly curved and glowing.

"Bite me, Uriel." Lucifer raised his hands, and a black cloud burst from them. Thousands of tiny, winged bugs swarmed the angel and took him down to the ground where the zombies went to town, jaws clacking.

As for Chris, he had no one to fight because, between his mom and dad and the damned undead, no one got near him.

But Isobel's family didn't have the same protection. *She'll kill me if they get hurt.*

Moving away from the circle of the dead, he shoved his way past them until he found the Rasputins...doing just fine on their own.

The elder Rasputin cackled as he flung lightning bolts into the sky, singeing feathers.

Thomas didn't fight at all, merely placed his hands on his wife's shoulders, and Chris could see the glow at the contact. As for Marya, she smiled as she chanted and twisted her hands. For a moment, Chris wondered what she did, and then he saw it, the green sprouting from the ground, spreading out tendrils ripe with thorns. The vines whipped into the sky, grabbing limbs and dragging the angels down. Thickets sprang up around the pair, protecting them from the undead.

They didn't need his help.

Heck, Chris didn't need help, for the dead didn't touch him. On the contrary, they parted for him and defended him; they protected him from the angels.

Because the angels were after him. And against the mindless dead, with only their rotting fingers, the tide turned against him.

Chris ducked and cursed as an angel swooped in close. Of all the times to not have a shovel handy. Standing back up, something clipped him, and his cheek throbbed. He raised a hand to his face, and it came away bloody.

"Did you have to hit the face?" he yelled. He'd not been blessed with many things growing up. Not a nice home. No regular meals or new clothes. All he had was his destiny—which didn't get him presents for Christmas—and his looks.

And now these angels, who he'd never done shit to, these sanctimonious pricks with their pretty little wings and their shiny swords—probably sold to them by Jesus himself—thought they could just swoop in and fuck over not only his face but also his sweet niece's party.

"That's fucking it," he roared. He clenched his fists and raised his head and let forth a mighty yell. When the next angel came in close, he swung, and...*thunk.*

A body hit the ground. Opening his eyes, he saw the strangest thing in his hand—a glowing fucking shovel outlined in a wispy gray light.

Not exactly his sister's flaming sword, but hot damn, he had his own magical weapon. He wasted no time using it, batting angels out of the sky, accidentally clipping some of the zombies who got in his way.

To his surprise, he found himself flanked—Mother on one side, Dad on the other, and his sister at his back.

His other sister, Bambi, held a stiletto and threatened anyone who got near War, as if that behemoth in a red suit needed help. War swung his mighty battle-ax and laughed. Was it wrong that the man, er, thing, er, horseman was growing on Chris?

The tide of the battle turned, and things became less chaotic. Chris actually got to look around, and it was then that he saw him.

His uncle. God.

Chris paused and looked him in the face. A countenance that should have been benevolent. A face he'd never met because he'd never had the chance.

Stalking close, God stood his ground, hands folded over his stomach, his expression calm.

"Why?" Chris asked. What had he ever done to earn his uncle's hatred? Couldn't they have talked things out? Did it have to come to war?

"You are sin." The words boomed out of God, and Chris gaped at him.

"What the fuck is that supposed to mean? I am sin. I'm just a guy, who happens to have the Devil as a father."

"You are King of Hell, the Destroyer of Nations. Your army is a perversion of mankind. Your very existence a stain upon this world."

"Wow, dude, whatever happened to turning the other cheek and all that forgiveness shit your church is always spouting about?"

"That is for the mortals. You are an abomination and must be destroyed!" The words exhaled out of God, who gleamed with all his might. The zealous righteousness of his quest shone from his eyes. His fierce determination was in the set of his jaw. "Seize the abomination."

Apparently, that meant Chris.

Somehow, his allies were torn from his side, and despite his mighty shovel, Chris proved too slow. Angels piled onto him, grabbed hold of his limbs, and took him to the ground. With their numbers and weight, they held Chris pinned and helpless. The only thing he could do was gaze up at God, who showed no mercy.

Wouldn't you know, though, his uncle was too

much of a pussy to strike the killing blow. His archangel Michael was instantly by his side.

Michael raised his sword, the blade humming with power, glowing white with heavenly fire. He held it high above his head and waited for the command.

The end had come. Not the one Chris had hoped for. At least Isobel wouldn't have to see it. He just wished he'd gotten to say how sorry he was for lying to her. To tell her one last time how much he loved her and how he wished they had more time.

"Do it," God ordered.

As the sword began its descent, Chris just hoped he could be manly about his death and not blubber if it hurt.

Before the sword could strike, his mother stepped in front of him, the scent of the grave following her.

A comforting smell. An unexpected rescue because she took the blow meant for him.

"Mother!" he gasped as she staggered back, the glowing sword stuck in her side.

Chris scrambled to his feet, not knowing what to do as Morgana swayed, all her crimes forgotten in that moment of selflessness.

But his mother didn't look at him, and it wasn't her wound that proved most shocking, but her next words as she stared at God. "You. I know you."

Elyon eyed her up and down, disapproval in his expression. "I highly doubt that. I do not consort with your type."

"My type?" Morgana laughed. "What a strange turn of events. I know you in spite of the face you now wear. You cannot hide your scent. And I've grown wiser since we last met."

God tugged his beard. "You are speaking nonsense, female. I don't know you."

Lie. Was Chris the only one who heard it?

"You do know me, and now I understand why your brother doesn't remember me."

Apparently, it was possible for God to blanch even whiter than he already was. He blustered. "I don't know what the whore speaks of. Michael, kill the witch. Run her through with your heavenly sword. She must be destroyed. She is evil incarnate."

But it was Chris's turn to save her. He stepped in front of his mother, raised his magical shovel, and said, "Don't you dare. Let her speak. Let us hear what she has to say."

The dead crowded close, and the angels—their faces twisted in disgust—moved aside. An army waiting for orders. Listening to the unfolding drama.

"What are you afraid of, Accolon?" Mother taunted. "At least that's what you called yourself back then. I should have listened to Merlin when he told me you were hiding something. Those clues you left, they were clever. They fooled me at the time, made me believe you were another in disguise," she said, her breath hitching, the sword still dangling from her side. "But the scent doesn't lie, and I can now see your aura.

The same one you had back then. It was you, not Lucifer, who bedded me. You, not he, who fathered my son."

And then, instead of a mic, his mother dropped.

26

THE SILENCE FELL SUDDENLY, the shock of Morgana's words stilling all motion, all fight, even breath. No one dared to make a sound as all eyes and ears were tuned to the drama unfolding.

Not liking it one bit, and used to being the center of attention, Lucifer farted. Didn't excuse himself, though, because that would be polite. It meant some gazes turned to him, which was better because, hello, most important person in the yard.

"I think you need to repeat that for everyone to hear, Morgana, because if I heard you right, you just said I'm not the daddy. You hear that, woman?" And by woman, he meant his wife, who'd given him hell when she found out he had a bastard son. "It wasn't me!"

"She's lying," blustered his brother. "The Antichrist is the spitting image of you."

"He is," Lucifer agreed, looking over at the boy who appeared quite shell-shocked, unlike his daughter, Bambi, who snickered. "Carries the family gene, too. Even got our Daddy's eyes." Not that he remembered much of his father. Atlas had long ago left this world for one that didn't weigh as heavily upon his shoulders.

"The idea I'm his father is preposterous. I took a vow of celibacy," Elyon said, a bead of sweat rolling down from his temple.

"Did you or didn't you bed my mother?" Chris found the balls to ask.

The longer his brother kept his lips clamped, the more Lucifer narrowed his gaze.

But it was Morgana, lying on the ground, gray smoke spilling from her injured side that spat, "Don't you dare try and wiggle out of this again. You knew you got me pregnant." Her gaze lasered Elyon. "I told you all those centuries ago I carried a child, your child, and then you disappeared. Hid from your responsibility."

More than one set of eyes rounded, and a shocked, "Ooooh!" went through the crowd. Lucifer wished he had some popcorn.

For his part, Elyon tried to appear innocent. "I wasn't your only lover. You were married to that king."

Which caused more than one of the heavenly host to step back, their faces twisted in disgust.

Playing the blame and shame game. Lucifer would have none of it. "Did you fornicate with the nice, married lady?"

"A few times. But I pulled out, each time." God told the truth.

But Morgana wasn't letting him off easy. "You pulled out after you started ejaculating, you idiot. Then, when I missed my menses and Merlin told me I was pregnant, you wouldn't see me. Told your buddy Peter in the barracks to turn me away when I came looking for you."

"I wasn't ready to settle down. Especially not with a sinful witch." Elyon sniffed, his expression ripe with contempt. "And I was right about you being the wrong sort. Look at what happened next. When I refused to consort with you further, you went on a rampage, laying waste to the land."

"Because I was angry," Morgana snapped, reviving enough to push herself up on her arms. "I was pregnant and hormonal, and what did you do? You had me locked away by your brother, but only after you had Merlin tell me those lies."

A mighty frown drew Lucifer's brows together into a slash. "What lies did Merlin spread?"

"My mentor said it was the Devil who impregnated me. Gullible fool that I was, I believed him." Morgana's lips pressed tight. "I should have known he lied. I knew there was something off about Accolon. Something good." Her lip curled into a sneer. "But I was younger then. Stupid, too. No wonder you wanted me locked away. If the world were to know you pulled another Mary, you would have lost all your followers."

"Brother, that is devious." Lucifer clapped his hands in admiration. "And to think, not only did you, as an imposter, impregnate the witch, you were also the one who devised the plan to lock her away. You set her up. You set us all up. Bravo!" Lucifer bowed in homage to the insidious plot.

For his part, Elyon appeared quite appalled. "I didn't lie. I merely ensured a danger to my flock—"

"Don't you mean danger to your dick? Can't exactly preach one man, one woman, and together forever 'til death do us part if you cast her aside, eh." Lucifer winked. "Damn if I don't feel close to you suddenly, brother. I always knew you had a bit of the Devil inside you."

"Don't compare me to you," Elyon boomed. "I am nothing like you."

"Me thinks he doth protest too much. About time you showed you weren't perfect."

"I am without sin."

"Lie," Lucifer announced with glee. "And you know what your religion says about liars."

"I am the Almighty Creator, the one true God. I can—hey, let go of me." Michael and the archangel Raphael gripped Elyon by his upper arms. "What are you doing? Unhand me."

"Sorry, my lord, but you'll have to come with us. By your own laws, you must repent."

Elyon's eyes widened. "You can't do this."

Except the angels, sworn to uphold God's rules,

could. They took him away in a cloud of white wings. Took Elyon to Heaven to pay penance and repent for his sins, their sudden departure meaning there was an army of the dead with no one to fight.

And a boy who wasn't his son standing with a dazed look in his eyes.

Chris sounded shell-shocked as he said, "God's my father."

"Who art in Heaven. Yada. Yada. We know." Lucifer snapped his fingers. "Which means, you need to change your last name. Can't have you besmirching my disreputable honor with good deeds and whatnot."

"I'm not the Antichrist," the boy repeated, obviously dense. A result of less-than-perfect genes.

Not his problem. Not anymore. "Well, this was fun. Muriel, thank you for a most excellent party. I'll have Lucinda's gift transported shortly. Now, you can all clean up without me. I must be off because, according to my baby pager"—he held up a vibrating seashell—"Gaia's going into labor. I'm gonna be a daddy again! Which means I need to grab some Cubans from Hell for some fresh-rolled cigars. Happy sinning!" With a final smirk, Lucifer left.

Apocalypse averted. Now on to the next calamity. Seeing his wife's hooha stretch in ways it shouldn't unless it was for his cock.

THE MOMENT HIS DAD, ahem, uncle left, Chris dropped to his knees. "Mother?" Despite all the shocking news, he didn't forget what she'd done.

She'd taken a blow meant for him. She cared.

Her dark gaze fixed on his face. "Don't you dare start blubbering. I'm dying; it's not a big deal."

"I thought you couldn't die."

"The demise of this form only means I shall transcend."

"But what if I don't want you to go?" He'd never given her a chance. He'd spent so much time hating her that he never even tried to get to know her.

"You have no choice. This body is weak. Too weak for this..." She let her hand fall from her side, and the gray mist thickened as it poured. "Just do me a favor. Don't forget me."

How could he? His mother was Morgana Le Fay. He grabbed her hand. "I won't."

"Good." She closed her eyes, and then she was gone, her body collapsing inward as if the mist were the only thing keeping it inflated.

He remained kneeling until Muriel tapped his shoulder. "Um, Chris. I know you're probably kind of grieving right now, but think you can do something about the dead bodies in my yard?"

"The bodies can wait," screeched Marya. "He has to go after my daughter. Isobel has been kidnapped!"

The words galvanized him like nothing else could. He jumped to his feet. "What do you mean she's been kidnapped?" Last he'd seen her, she'd gone into the house to pee. And...never came back. Not even to fight. Isobel would never shy away from a fight.

His blood ran colder than a corpse.

Dashing into the house, he called for her to no avail. He made it to the front door and sprinted out onto the driveway. Still nothing.

She was gone.

She was...

"*Woof.*"

Goshen sat on the driveway, barking.

Chris raised his head until he could see why.

A chariot, white and gleaming, drawn by bloody flying horses, came prancing into view. Holding the reins, Jesus. Falling out of the chariot?

"Shit. Isobel." Chris began to run, arms outstretched, not fast enough, not going to make it.

With a mighty push of his hind legs, Goshen leapt into the air. Isobel grabbed hold of his fur, and they both landed, safe and sound.

But Chris still yelled, "Jesus Christ, get your ass back here so I can beat you senseless."

"No time, brother." Jesus circled the chariot in the sky. "I just heard the news. God's going to jail for a few centuries, which means I get to be in charge. Finally." Jesus fist-pumped.

"I don't give a shit about that. You took my wife."

"And I brought her back. After all, being with my brother's wife would be a sin."

Brother?

Ah, fuck.

"Pop into Heaven when you get a chance to say hi. I'll tell Peter at the gates to let you in." With a wave, Jesus flew off, and Chris was left standing, jaw dropped.

A body hurtled into him. The dog. Who put him flat on his back and licked him.

"Argh, dog slobber," he yelled.

Only to get crushed a second time, this time by a pleasant weight. "Chris, you're all right." Isobel plastered him with womanly slobber, which he didn't mind at all.

"I don't know what I am right now," he said, still trying to catch his breath. "The Devil isn't my father."

"I heard. But, guess what. I'm—"

"Uncle Chris!" Lucinda squealed his name as she came barreling out of the house. "It's time for my cake."

Cake? Who wanted cake when their whole world had just crumbled?

Except...the world wasn't ending.

Mother was dead. And when he returned to the yard, the undead were cleaning themselves up. Shuffling away, going to their final rest—*until I need to call them again anyway.*

The tent was torn to shit, but the sun had gone down sometime during the battle.

And sure enough, when he emerged into the yard, Nefertiti held a cake with a handful of candles aloft. Everyone began to sing.

The end of a prophecy celebrated with chocolate cake.

As the party wound down, he looked to see Lucinda napping on Auric's lap, Muriel snuggled by his side. Bambi had claimed War's mighty thighs, and Chris looked away when he saw where the horseman's hand was creeping. Death and Pestilence were off in a corner making out. Famine was eating the leftovers, and as for the Rasputins, they asked Chris and Isobel for a ride home.

Home? Where was home? Not in Hell. The moment Chris found out the truth, he knew he couldn't keep the crown. A silver lining in all this mess.

He struggled to his feet. "Let me find a phone so I can call us a cab. I guess to get to the airport."

"No planes." Rasputin shook his head. "Fucking metal deathtraps."

"I am not driving twenty fucking hours, old man," Chris grumbled.

"No driving either. Just do it," the old wizard said.

"Do what?" Chris asked.

"Make a portal."

"I can't." Always his first words of choice.

Only Isobel whispered, "Yes, you can. Remember what Muriel did?"

Yeah, as a matter of fact, he did. He'd watched as she made a portal. Saw the magic. A lot of it.

"I don't know if I can do it."

"I know you can. With my help."

She placed her hands on him, and he concentrated, concentrated, pulled at the power, let it pool inside, then stumbled. What next?

"Picture the house," Isobel whispered. "Fix it in your mind and then rip open the space between here and there."

Rip open the space. Because that was so easy. He didn't believe it would work. But he couldn't *not* try— not with everyone watching.

What if I fail?

"There is no room for pessimism, only greatness." Funny how that sounded like his mother.

He squinted, picturing the house, the windows, the door, the yard.

Then, when he had it firmly fixed in his mind, he reached out and grabbed hold of reality and tore it open.

A portal formed.

He gaped. "Holy shit. I did it." But did it work? Goshen woofed and then leapt through the hole. Rasputin and the others followed. Leaving Isobel and Chris.

"What if it doesn't go home?" he said, voicing his worry aloud. What if he'd just sent her entire family off into oblivion?

"I believe in you." The most powerful words ever. Followed by her faith. She stepped through the rip, and since he couldn't live without her, he stepped through, too.

CHRIS TOOK THEM HOME. Their home, not her parents', which caused some grumbling.

Rasputin wasn't enamored with the idea of taking an Uber back to the house, but her daddy convinced him, saying Grandfather could walk if he didn't like it.

When the car pulled into the driveway and the moment to say goodbye arrived, Isobel couldn't help but hug her father tightly. Eyes wet. Heart aching. "I missed you so much."

"As did I," he whispered against her hair. "But I would do it again if I thought it would spare your life."

Because in that awkward spell as they waited for the Uber pickup, she'd finally learned the truth. How her daddy had used his own soul to try and keep Morgana in prison. Only to have her mother set them both free because she had a different plan. A plan that ended up working out for almost all of them. She couldn't help feeling a pang for Chris, who'd realized his mother truly did care for him, only to lose her in the same moment. But that didn't negate her happiness at having her father back.

She squeezed him, and her voice was tight as she said, "I'm glad you're back."

"Me, too."

As for Mother, she sniffed. "Dinner. Sunday. No excuses. Wear something without holes." Which was her way of saying "I love you."

As for Grandfather, he cackled. "Best party I've attended in ages."

After they'd left, she and Chris stood for a moment in their front yard, the silence enveloping them, the mist rising from the ground obscuring the world.

Only they existed.

"What a day," he finally said.

"Let's go to bed." She tugged him into the house, but before hitting the bedroom, she detoured for a shower. Chris held himself stiff, shock still running through his veins.

She knew how to loosen him up. She ran soapy hands over his muscled frame. Cleansed the battle from his skin. Woke other parts of him and reminded him that there was pleasure to be had in the land of the living.

When she dropped to her knees and worshipped him, he let loose a long sigh.

"I love you, Isobel."

So did she. And she proved it. True love always swallowed.

They made it to bed and made love again, softly, gently, an exploration of each other's bodies that reminded them that they'd survived the apocalypse. They'd managed to circumvent fate and death.

They held each other after, their bodies damp, their breathing ragged, their privacy broken by an intruding voice.

"I should have known you weren't my son. Not dirty enough in the bedroom."

Isobel squeaked at the intruder and hid under the sheets, whereas Chris sighed. "For fuck's sake, don't you have anything better to do than harass me?"

Lucifer perched at the foot of the bed, leering at them. "Gaia and the new baby are having a nap. So I thought I'd pop in and tell you that you're fired."

"Too late. I quit."

"You can't quit. The job doesn't work that way."

"The job should have never been mine to start with. I'm not your son," Chris retorted. "So take back your damned throne. I never want to see Hell again."

"And you won't. Son of God." Lucifer snickered.

Chris groaned. "Don't remind me."

"Speaking of reminders, Rasputin said to tell you that he's invited the horsemen to stay with them for a while. Apparently, your mother had them living out of a motel by the highway."

"What?" The statement caused Isobel to scramble

into a seated position while clutching the sheet to her chest. "Why can't they stay with you?"

"Because they were never my soldiers. Not even truly Morgana's. They are the servants of prophecy. They will only ride when the Fates call them."

"And what do the Fates say now?" Chris asked.

"Is it over?" Isobel asked.

"Is what over?" Lucifer queried instead. "Life is a never-ending series of battles and confrontations and choices. When one ends, another begins."

"That's pretty Zen shit for the Devil." Chris scrubbed a hand through his hair.

"Practicing for the baby," Lucifer remarked. "Congratulate me. I am a father."

"Poor little shit. He has my condolences."

The Devil chuckled. "Elyon might have fathered you, but that's definitely a hint of my humor. I'll be sure to rub that in his face when I visit him in prison."

"Waa. Waa. Waa."

The ghostly cry emerged from nowhere and yet was everywhere. Isobel snuggled closer to Chris while Lucifer scowled.

"Guess that's my cue to leave. Feel free to sin some more."

"We're married. It's allowed." Isobel enjoyed rubbing the salt into that one, especially since Lucifer winced as he faded out of sight.

Beside her, Chris lost the rigid tension in his body.

"Fuck me, but now that he's not my dad, I kind of miss him. At least he kind of paid me attention."

Given what Isobel knew of Charlie's upbringing, she knew Elyon wouldn't do the same. "At least you know the truth. Crazy business. Who would have thought we'd be on the side that ended up saving the world?"

"Not that crazy, considering I was never who people thought I was."

"But it's not like you're a nobody."

Chris made a moue of displeasure. "Honestly, given the choice between Son of God and the Devil, can I select none of the above?"

"How do you think I feel? God is your father, and the Devil is your uncle. And Jesus is your brother."

"Who's in love with my wife."

"Can you blame him?" She arched a brow. "I am pretty awesome. And don't forget, you're still cousins with Muriel and Bambi."

"I don't need you to recite all my family connections. I'm aware of who is who. I'm just not me anymore. What happens now?" he asked, looking at Isobel. "If I'm not the Antichrist, destined to rule the world, then what does that leave?"

"Anything you want. You can be anyone. Go anywhere."

"Go somewhere else?" he mused aloud. "Enter the unknown?"

"Embark on an adventure. Find a new home. One

for you, me, Goshen, and the baby." She placed his hand on her stomach.

He didn't freak out. Rather smiled. "Our child." He flexed his fingers. "War doth fly on the wings of the future. The blood of the innocents shall soak the Earth and give rise to a new dominion."

"What the heck is that supposed to mean?"

Chris turned a smile on her. "This is not the end."

LATER THAT SAME NIGHT, LUCINDA SLIPPED OUT of bed and into the backyard. Despite being hidden in the vault at the time, she knelt in the exact spot where Morgana had dissolved into nothingness.

Except nothing ever completely disappeared. Sometimes, it just lost cohesion for a bit. Lucinda gathered the tiny motes of Morgana's spirit. She spilled the pieces into the pink amulet. For a moment, it glowed in the darkness, and a cool breeze, hinting of death, lifted Lucinda's hair.

This was not the end.

EPILOGUE

The apocalypse didn't end things as the seers had predicted. The world emerged in a bit of a mess, but humanity had a way of persevering. Much like the days and months and years after the Flood, the humans rebuilt. They multiplied. They sinned...

The backlog in Hell was still pretty huge. That lazy nephew of his really lacked an efficient bone in his body. But Lucifer welcomed the work, given Gaia had this thing about sharing the duties with the new baby—who seemed to shit and scream an awful lot. The office was a place to escape and have a cigar, throw on the telly, and grab a few winks under the guise of work.

But he couldn't hide from his fatherly duties all the time. When he went home to his suite in the tower, the first thing Gaia did when he walked through the door was thrust the baby at him and declare, "Your turn."

Holding his new son in his arms, his only son,

Lucifer stared at the tiny face with its big eyes staring back at him. The depths of them dancing with flames, a family trait.

He thought about strangling the fragile little neck. Smothering that Cupid's-bow mouth. He could toss the baby in the Styx. Leave it in the wild. All manner of things he could—and should—do to the one and only Antichrist. The real one this time. The one the prophecies truly spoke about.

Except...what if they were wrong?

What if I kill the only hope we have for a future?

Because, after all, he had let Lucinda—named *abomination* by more than one seer—live.

"You, my son, will do great things in this world," he crooned. "But if you ever come after me or the crown, I'll end you." Because in a world that consisted of me myself and I, there was room for only one Dark Lord, one King of the Underworld. *And my vacation is over, sinners, so prepare yourself, because your turn is coming soon.*

The End

But I doubt we've seen the last of Lucifer and Hell.

Curious about the other stories in the Hell series. Then check out:

Princess of Hell with Lucifer's Daughter, Snowballs in Hell, Hell's Revenge, Vacation Hell

Welcome to Hell includes A Demon and his Witch, A Demon and his Psycho, Date with Death, A Demon and her Scot, Hell's Kitty, Hell's Geek, Hell's Bells

Wickedest Witch (standalone but related to Hell's Son series)

Last Minion Standing (standalone)

CPSIA information can be obtained
at www.ICGtesting.com
Printed in the USA
LVHW091627301018
595356LV00002B/367/P